HIDEOUS

A Dark Erotic Romance

Hideous is a work of fiction intended for mature readers. All sexually active characters are fictional and are over the age of 18 years. Names, characters, places, and incidents are either the product of the author's imagination or are used fictitiously. Any resemblance to actual persons, living or dead, events, or locales is entirely coincidental.

ISBN: 9798697034828

The Butte Trail of Pilot Mountain is one of my favorite places in the world.

But it's the last place I should be after dark.

And when a deranged psycho starts chasing me, I know I'm fucked.

But then a hooded stranger saves me on the brink of a brutal assault, and has his men take me somewhere "safe," which really amounts to nothing more than a dark room with a dog bed to sleep on.

It's this same dark room where the hooded stranger treats me like a dog, calling me with the snap of a finger and placing a leash and collar around my neck. He refuses to speak to me, or show me his face.

I'm told that I wanted this all along.

But it isn't what I wanted. It was all just a misunderstanding.

A misunderstanding that comes from a dark part of my past. A part that I regret.

A part that almost cost me my life.

A part I thought was over.

But it isn't.

And it won't be over until someone dies...

Table of Contents

One... 1

Two 12

Seven months ago~Leigh 23

Three...29

Six months ago~Leigh 36

Four 38

Five months ago~Leigh 46

Five 50

Four months ago~Leigh 64

Six 69

Four months ago~Leigh 84

Seven.. 88

Four months ago~Leigh 104

Eight.. 107

Three and a half months ago~Jack 120

Nine 128

Three months ago~Jack 162

Ten 171

Eleven 187

Twelve...206

Thirteen 228

Fourteen 244

Fifteen..268

Other books by Brittany Adams: 283

About the Author.......................................284

Twist your fingers through mine.

Feel the fire on my skin, see the rage in my eyes.

Kiss me.

Taste the madness of my mind.

One

Blackness engulfs me as I choke on the cool air. I pull in a raspy breath, my throat constricting as I dart my gaze around the woods in a frantic search. A thick haze swirls around the trees that surround me. Beyond that, it's too dark to see.

Does it really take one split-second decision to completely flip your life end over end?

It does.

I should *not* have come back here to look for my damn phone.

My pulse thrums in my ears. I death-grip the flashlight that's no longer on, and I'm torn between running—throttling myself further from civilization—and staying put. Maybe he gave up. Why keep running if he's no longer chasing me?

My breathing steadies but pierces the silence, harmonizing with the *thud-thud-thud* in my ears. A fine mist billows out of my lungs with each exhale. I hold. Wait. Already wondering how long I will stay fixed to this spot. My feet are like lead weights, vibrating as they sink into the ground, frozen.

I think about the last thing I ate today: a Caesar salad for lunch eight hours ago. I always put on extra croutons because a salad isn't a salad without seasoned bread. I wonder how much those croutons have digested or if they're nothing more than chunks of swollen dough the ME will find during my autopsy.

I should have called Andrea from a payphone, told her I was coming here to find my cellphone that I lost earlier while hiking. I'm way the fuck off-trail at this point. And without my phone, I sure as shit can't call her. Or 911.

I divert my attention back to my stalker. Is that what he's called? He's only been chasing me for a few minutes. Is there a certain length of time someone has to be after you before they qualify as a stalker? I can't allow these thoughts to enter my head. Survivors act on instinct, not by thinking about their death before it occurs.

I don't know what he wants from me, but I'm pretty sure he isn't selling candy bars for a fundraiser or in need of directions to the local church.

It was his laughter that alerted me to his presence. One of those deep belly laughs that had a fevered pitch to it. The kind of laugh when you're the only one amused. And it was through that laughter he made an announcement: he was going to get me. Catch up to me. Find me.

Walking along the Butte Trail at Pilot Mountain after the sun has set to find a lost phone isn't the smartest thing I've done. And now I'm fucked since this son of a bitch has decided to join me on my late-night stroll through the woods.

I am at an advantage, though. I've hiked this trail probably hundreds of times over the years. I know every step, every rock, and every stick like the back of my hand. Problem is, like I said, I'm off-trail, which is a dangerous place to be. Footing is unsteady and hills and cliffs abound. I know about where the drop-offs are, and obviously I'm avoiding them as evidenced by my still being alive and *not* at the base of this mountain. But I don't know how much longer I can keep running from a deranged man without teetering off the edge of a rock. My only hope is that, if I do, I take him with me.

I do another visual sweep, my ears pricking like a dog's when I hear a noise. It could be nothing—a leaf falling, a squirrel nesting. I hold my breath, the air growing cold and heavy around me.

He could be right there.

I feel dizzy. My gut twists. My body shudders from a chill. A burn rises in my throat. And a whistle sounds way in the distance.

My body lurches but I stop myself. Running will make too much noise.

I hold for another beat, my breath smoky.

But then a twig snaps, closer this time. Leaves crunch underfoot. A cold wind blows. He swears under his breath.

I narrow my eyes and see him. He's holding something. A long stick or a shovel.

Oh god. A shovel?

My breath hitches in my throat. The led weights at the bottom of my legs are light once again, pushing off the ground and launching me forward. My vision is obscured by the haze in the air, so speed isn't much of an option now. Fuck, I never should have stopped.

I'm vocal now, panic overwhelming me as I realize it's too late. Involuntary whimpers escape my throat as I move as quickly as possible, hoping I don't trip and fall. I briefly entertain the thought that it may be less torturous for me to turn around and face him, just get this over with.

But my stalker makes that decision for me.

His footsteps are right behind me. A hand on my shoulder makes me jerk. I flail my arms wide as the shovel handle is wedged against my throat. And then my plastic flashlight goes falling to the ground.

I reach up and grab the wood, coughing and sputtering violently as the pressure builds against my neck.

"Told you I'd get you." His lips tickle my ear, his breath coffee-sour. The rest of him smells like fried fish.

I tug on the stick as hard as I can, struggling to breathe.

The stranger hitches his knee against my ass and lunges me forward, smashing me against a tree. He pushes my head against the bark and slides the handle out of the way before pressing his body against mine. The bark scratches my face, burning my flesh as it scrapes my cheeks. I press my palms against the rough surface.

"Please ..." My voice is tight and shaky as I beg. "What do you want?"

He sniffs me, filling his lungs with my scent. My brow narrows as I attempt to twist my head around and look at him. I need to see what he looks like, his expression, as if it will somehow give answers to my fate.

"You don't want me to answer that," he snarls. His voice is higher than it was seconds ago.

A tightness spreads through my chest. Evil incarnate is here and he has spoken.

Before I have a chance to process the hundreds of thoughts that are flipping through my mind, he's pulled my hands away from the tree and kicked my legs out from underneath me. I crash to the ground, a rock nailing me in the ribs and knocking the breath out of me.

Panic seizes me as I struggle to expand my lungs. My nails dig into the leaves below as I push upward. A blow to my back sends me reeling, the pain so intense it radiates all the way to my toes. I open my mouth to scream but nothing comes out because my chest is still paralyzed. The blood in my body runs ice cold.

He sits on my upper back, his weight crushing. I feel him moving on top of me as I lie across dirt and sticks and leaves. The earth is letting him hurt me. The silence is letting him take me. And after years of giving me the solitude I needed, this trail is betraying me with that same solitude. Where's my white knight when I fucking need him?

He tugs at the waist of my jeans, jerking them down below my buttocks, and then further still until they're around my ankles.

I still can't breathe but unconsciousness would be a gift. I can see the rings of darkness encircle my vision as he rotates on top of me. My body warms, my blood now fizzing like hot soda through my veins. Noises fade into the background as I start to slip away.

I fist a handful of leaves as I silently pray that this will be the worst of it.

That I won't be awake for any of it.

That he will have mercy on me and leave me here when he's finished.

His hands grope my ass, and my eyes close.

And then, a crack whips in the air. A loud snap like a tree falling in the distance. Except I'm pretty sure it's coming from right above me. His weight jerks on top of me, and then another crackling sound, this one like bones snapping.

His body falls to the ground next to me, the thump sounding like dead weight. I pull in a rush of air, my lungs expanding once again and sending cool waves rippling through my chest and abdomen. Confused but relieved, I roll onto my back, the pain jabbing me then disappearing quickly. I sit up and reach for my pants and see movement out of the corner of my eye, so I snap my head to the side.

Clouds drag across the moon, its light burning the cold fog. The air clears as my eyes adjust to the figure in the woods.

He's darker than the night itself. A long black cape flows around him, a hood obscuring his face. He holds the stick that was just wedged against my neck and compressing my trachea. It's narrow at one end and wide at the other, like a rifle.

I look at my assailant laid out next to me. His arms are tossed above his head, and his jeans are unzipped.

My gut twists, and I lean down to pull up my pants, getting on my knees to button them back.

The caped figure stands still, watching me. My heart thrums.

"Who ... who are you?"

I scoot back against the tree behind me and hug my chest. I assume he's not the enemy. I mean, he just saved my life. Why would he do that just to kill me?

The figure turns his head to the side and flicks it down, nodding once. Several men emerge from the darkness as though appearing from thin air. The figure takes one step toward me. For a second, I think I will see his face, see just exactly who this dark hero is. But then a cool wind blows and his hands rise up. His cape swings out, rising in a circle before he disappears. I swallow hard as one of his men approaches me.

"It's not safe here, Leigh. You must come with us."

He extends his hand to me and I coil. Not because he's a stranger but because of the accent. I don't have a problem with foreigners, but he sounds vaguely Russian, and we don't have a whole lot of Russians around here in this rural southern town. Needless to say, the word "mafia" quickly comes to mind.

I flick my gaze behind him, the caped man now a small shadow as he fades into the woods. "How do you know my name? Who are you people?" I ask.

Seriously. Why is the Butte Trail suddenly swarming with men?

He kneels in front of me and clasps his hands, his rugged face laced with a mixture of compassion and impatience.

"I will tell you. But you must come with me if you want to live to see tomorrow."

I cast one last glance at my attacker lying deathly still before I finally stand up.

"I want to live," I answer.

But I'm not sure if going with him is a good idea. Can I tell him thanks but no thanks? Somehow, I don't think that's an option.

Two

Russia leads me through the woods, shining a high-powered flashlight as we forge ahead from where we were, where my attacker is. The other two men are behind us, their presence oddly comforting.

I know there's another parking lot around here somewhere, near the knob of Pilot Mountain and the start of the Jomeokee Trail. Since the clouds have cleared, I can make out the swell of the peak, even in the darkness. My ex used to call it Mount Nipple because that's what it looks like: the tip of a breast poking up into the southern sky. If he were still alive, and if things hadn't ended the way they had, I would be tempted to call him right now. If I had my damn phone.

"Are we headed towards the Service Road parking lot?" I ask. "I'm kind of turned around here."

He uses his flashlight to swing at some hanging limbs, moving them out of our way. "We are going somewhere safe. Please, don't worry. No one can hurt you now."

"Yeah, I get that. It's just … my car's on Service Road. I'd like to head home and put this night behind me."

I'm not heading home. Fuck that shit. I'm going straight to the police and telling them what just happened. As of recently, I'm not one of those who bottles everything inside because I'm ashamed or scared or hurt. That mother fucker attacked me, and if he's still alive, I'll be damned if I let him get away with it and do it to someone else. But I don't feel comfortable talking openly with Russia. I'm not sure how he would react to me bringing the cops into what went down here tonight.

"You will be safe." He turns his head to the side, his voice monotone as he answers me. "Do not worry, *fetita*."

We amble on, my thoughts continuously returning to the caped man. And I feel increasingly uncomfortable the further we go. I think of how fucked up this situation is, that I've been rescued by a group of men whom I now have no choice but to let lead me through the woods, in the dark.

How do I know this isn't a setup? That this attack wasn't arranged by the mafia, and they're simply going to try to wear me down, make me more vulnerable than before?

We'll save her from her attacker, forcing her to trust us. Then we'll come at her when she least expects it.

Yeah, see? Fucked.

But nothing else makes sense. How did these guys even know he was out here? That *we* were out here and that I was in danger? No one is supposed to be on this trail after dark. Granted, it's only around nine o'clock or so. But we're far away from the city limits, practically in the middle of nowhere. What the hell were these guys doing out here?

And why can I not stop thinking about the man in the dark cape?

I'm afraid to ask, so maybe I am a little scared. But when I hear the sounds of wheels whirring along the pavement, I feel a rush of relief.

Russia starts speaking his native language, and the men who moments ago had my back now rush ahead of me. They talk for several minutes as I stand there, trying to figure out what language they're speaking. I spin in a circle when I hear a noise, completely and utterly freaked out at this point. My gaze is pulled to the trees above, the limbs gently painting the sky as a cool wind blows.

"Go! Go!" Russia hurries the men along, sweeping his arm to the side. The men shine their flashlights ahead, cutting through the trees and disappearing out of sight.

"Where are they going?" I don't like the thought of being alone with this guy. He hasn't exactly given me a reason to distrust him, but since there's safety in numbers—even when those numbers are strangers—I'd rather they stick around.

He twists his head to the side and holds up a finger, telling me to wait. Moments later, I hear a chirp, and Russia nods, waving me forward as he starts to walk again.

"They are ensuring our safety."

I take a few quick steps to catch up to Russia, the road ahead coming into view.

"Why do we need to be concerned about safety? And you told me you would tell me who you were." I'm starting to get impatient. With adrenaline still coursing through my veins, I want answers right now.

Russia pauses as we stand at the edge of the pavement. The full moon above is bright, illuminating the street that glints small slivers of rock. A black sedan is parked ahead of us, on the other side of the road in a patch of grass. I look to either side, noticing that not a soul is in sight. No houses, no cars, and even the wind has died down, leaving me all alone in this night with strangers-*slash*-heroes.

"I will tell you what you need to know once we are inside car. But we must leave, immediately."

I grit my teeth, a part of me wanting to tell him that I'm not going anywhere with him unless he starts giving me answers. But I also know that I'm vulnerable right now, completely lost and at his mercy. So I pull in a deep breath and tell myself to chill the fuck out. If they were going to hurt me, they would have done so by now, right?

The sedan's headlights come on, brightening the black top ahead.

"Come, let's go."

He takes me by the hand and pulls me across the road. I shuffle forward but he stays several feet ahead of me, opening up the rear door and waiting for me to slip inside.

He slides in the seat next to me and the car moves forward. Russia puts on his seat belt as the interior lights slowly dim, then he looks at me, indicating I should do the same with a nod and a look.

I ignore him and lean forward to the driver. "My car's on Service Road. I'd appreciate a lift there."

He glances in the rearview mirror, angling his head to look at Russia. The man in the passenger seat pulls a breath mint out of his pocket and pops it in his mouth.

"It can't be far," I add. "You got a GPS or something?"

"I have failed to make myself clear," Russia says. "We are not going to this Service Road of yours. We are not going to your car. Boss wishes for you to be brought to his home where you are safe from predators."

I lean back in the seat and study him as best I can. We are literally in the middle of Nowhere, Bumfuckville, and back country roads are never lit with streetlights. Every few seconds, the moonlight casts through the trees, and I can see him strumming his fingers on his knee.

"What predators? I want answers. Now."

He leans toward the middle of the car and says something to the driver, who nods his head and touches the radio button. Smooth jazz comes on, making me nostalgic for my younger years. My dad used to listen to jazz every morning when he took me to school. It was the only way to block out my mother's screams echoing in my head. In both our heads.

"Your attack was no random act. He was going to hurt you. And there are others who wish the same ... *demise*. For you."

The air around me turns icy. My world spins.

"Who? Why?"

"Doesn't matter now," he answers. "Our job is to accompany boss. Take care of business. Clean up the mess."

A sharp pain shoots through my temples. I rub them, leaning forward until my head is resting against the cool leather. I don't even know what my demise was supposed to be. Rape? Assault? Death? My body shudders.

Clean up the mess.

"You don't know why I was attacked, but you knew to be there?"

He pulls in a long breath and twists in the seat to face me. "Listen to me and listen to me closely, *fetita*. There are things in life you have no control over. Sometimes, you are handed sack of gold bricks and luxurious mansion to live in, and all the jewels in the world. And other times, the great god of life spreads his ass open wide with fingers and takes giant shit on your face."

The man in the passenger seat snickers.

I stare at Russia as he continues. "When you are lucky, when you are very special, one great man comes along, a savior of sorts, and slams butt of rifle in god's skull, giving you … new rent on life. Do you understand?"

"It's *lease*, but yeah, I get it," I mutter.

Another thing I get is the distinct impression he doesn't want me questioning a thing. Or looking this gift horse in the mouth. He obviously doesn't know me because I've never been good at keeping my mouth shut. For long, anyway. Especially when I have about a hundred questions and none of them are being answered. Like, where is this savior, the one in the cape?

"So, basically, when you said you would tell me who you were, you were lying?"

"I said I would tell you what you needed to know. I have done that."

"Where is he? The one with the rifle. Is he your boss?"

He bobs his head once. "Yes, he is boss. And he will be home soon, preparing for you."

Nervousness channels through my gut, an unwelcome feeling when I'd rather be comforted in light of recent events.

"And where is home?"

We approach an oncoming car, the headlights illuminating Russia's face. He is looking at me, eyes tired, hair gray, lips parted.

"Get comfortable."

I start to tell him everything I'm thinking right now. Like the fact that people will be looking for me, that my phone is out there in the woods somewhere, tossed along the trail that leads right to the body of my attacker. And I think about lying, telling him that I'm related to someone really important who shares deeply rooted ties with the police department, and if anything happens to me, their asses will be lined up in front of a firing squad. Most southerners don't have trouble taking the law into their own hands, especially in my neck of the woods. Vigilantism is a *thing* out here. Something I haven't always been proud of, until this very moment.

But I am not related to anyone important. Mom's … gone. And so is my father. And if I have any surviving relatives, I'm sure they want nothing to do with me.

"I don't have a choice in this, do I?"

This time, I can feel the tension spilling from his body as he turns to me.

He pauses a moment, then shrugs and says, "You wanted this, Leigh."

I think it was the way he held his cigarette between his fingers that turned me on. It was all the way down, against the webbed flesh. I hate it when men hold their cigarettes up high near the fingernail. It's the smoking equivalent of sticking out your pinky when you're drinking tea.

The diamond in his ear glinted when he turned to look at me, the outdoor bar lights catching it just so. I had been watching him for a while, feeling my insides want to crumble at his hotness. Blond hair, blue eyes, and a hint of stubble that said *I got better shit to do than shave.*

And he didn't smile but I could tell by the way his brow twitched that he was imagining fucking me, imagining what it would be like.

He tipped his glass up, drank it down, and finally approached me.

"You're going to have to be a little more subtle." His voice was thick like black smoke.

"Why's that?" I asked him.

"Because the way you're looking at me, most men would assume you want to be taken out back and fucked behind the dumpsters." His eyes darted to my chest, then back up to my eyes.

I raised a brow, a little shocked at his forwardness. "Maybe that's what I want. Rough and dirty."

I could almost hear his dick pop under his jeans, flick against the denim. He sat next to me and picked up my drink before tipping it up and giving it a sniff. "Bay breeze?"

I nodded.

"How old are you?"

"Twenty-nine. You?"

He chuckled. "Thirty-two. Want another?"

I nodded again.

He waved to the bartender, ordered my third drink for the night.

"I'm Jack."

"Leigh," I said.

He passed me my drink, what was left of it, giving my face a once-over, like he wanted to be sure he was satisfied with his decision for the night. His eyes were big like blueberry saucers. I wanted to lick them, lick him all over. But instead, I picked up my bay breeze and guzzled the rest of it down.

"What do you do for fun, Leigh? Besides look for men in bars to fuck you behind dumpsters?"

I laughed, spraying my drink everywhere. The bartender looked at me, shook his head and tossed a towel in our direction. It landed in front of Jack.

Way to work for that tip, buddy.

I mumbled a *sorry* and wiped up my mess. Jack was smirking.

"Well, believe it or not, I don't hang out at bars a lot at all. My girlfriend is here on a blind date. Wanted me to come along in case things went awry."

"Oh?" He was already scoping the place, looking for Andrea. "Where is she?"

I flicked my thumb over my shoulder. "Over there, in the green dress."

He smirked. "Holy shit."

"What?" I turned around to look at her. She was sitting at the small round table, lip-locked with her date and groping his leg under the table. "Oh. Guess things are the opposite of awry."

"Does that mean you can go off duty?"

I snorted. "Yes. But I rode with her. So she better not ditch me."

"Maybe you can catch a ride home with someone else." He moved his hand under the bar, adjusted his jeans, shifted in the stool.

"Maybe I can." I finished the rest of my drink in one swallow right as the bartender brought me a fresh one.

"Good. I've always been a sucker for a blue-eyed brunette."

I smirked while doing this eye-roll thing. Like I've never heard that line before.

Jack smirked back and pulled a pack of cigarettes from the front pocket of his shirt. He shook it until a brown filter popped out, then passed it my way.

"You do know those things cause cancer, right?"

"A simple no would suffice. And fact: most people who have lung cancer don't smoke."

"Fact: that's actually a misleading fact. Most of those non-smokers are former smokers. Not to mention there are other things for which you can tip your hat to the good old cigarette, like COPD, emphysema, high blood pressure, heart attacks, high cholesterol, strokes, and mouth and throat cancer."

He slipped the brown filter between his lips, lit it with a zippo. Cancer-causing or not, I loved that sound. The smooth *chink* of metal on flint. And the way the smell of the butane mixed with the tobacco made my stomach hurt thinking of my dad.

Better days, easier times.

I watched Jack pull on his cigarette and blow the smoke out of the corner of his mouth without taking his eyes off me.

"Well, you're just a goddamn walking medical encyclopedia, aren't you, Leigh?" His smile let me know he wasn't pissed. I wasn't either. To me, that type of banter was foreplay. Sarcasm, arguing, letting me know you're not going to take my shit, all that.

"Stick with me. I'm a fountain of useful medical information."

Twenty minutes later, we were inside his truck. And I was on his lap, hugging the steering wheel while I rode his dick. Old leather and gas filled my nose as our flesh slapped together. Jack grunted, pounding up and down, his cock rubbing the swell of my G-spot. My shirt was bunched up high, and my tits rubbed along the smooth wheel as I came. His hands slid up my waist, cupped my tits, pinched my nipples. I bucked against his thrust.

"I think I like you, Leigh."

I felt his semen come out, felt the stickiness of it as it dripped out of me and slicked along my thighs.

And I kept my eyes focused on the dumpsters ahead, wondering if he'd ever fucked anyone behind them.

Three

I had asked Russia what he meant. That I had wanted this? How?

He didn't answer. Went back to *tap-tap-tapping* his fingers on his knees.

I give that a lot of thought in the car, how I could have wanted someone to violently attack me deep in the woods in the middle of the night. And I decide that it's a language barrier. That what he meant was I had asked for it the way a woman wearing a mini-skirt walking alone down a dark alley asks to be raped.

It's vile and disgusting and downright insulting. And it makes my blood boil. But I keep my mouth closed and don't say a word. What would be the point?

Within the hour, we're traveling over gravel, rocks crunching under the tires. My body and limbs are heavy as I sit up in the car, the pain from my assault coming in sharp waves as the adrenaline wears off. Russia is talking on the phone, his voice low and quiet as we stop in front of a large two-story stone house. Trees surround us on both sides—a fortress that makes me shudder and ensures that I don't even think of escaping.

"All right, you will come with me now." He opens the door and I slide out on his side, hugging myself. Despite my jacket, the cold cuts through me.

Walking me to the front door, Russia moves quickly. I expect to find my caped savior waiting for us at the door since this is his home, but he doesn't seem to be anywhere in sight, not even when we walk inside. But at least it's warm in here. Dark but warm.

"Follow me."

He zips around several corners, my eyes darting around the place. The house is spacious but sparingly decorated. We pass through a sitting room that boasts an entire wall of books that look older than I am. A brown leather wing-back chair rests in the corner, a small table next to it holding a vase with a single rose in full bloom, blood-red, the outer petals drooping.

I follow Russia down a barely illuminated hallway, candelabras mounted on the wall and casting a soft light that mists out every few feet.

"I believe you will find your accommodations comfortable." He pushes open a door, and as I walk in, I'm taken aback at how little I see. These can't possibly be my accommodations. "You have everything you need here."

I stare at him blankly. "I don't even remotely have everything I need here."

I glance up at the ceiling. A portrait of a nude is painted on the plaster, her body enveloped in chains, her face smiling in ecstasy.

Ignoring my comment, Russia walks to a door in the corner, pushing it open. "You have full bath, plenty of towels, new toothbrush, and all amenities." He walks back to the entryway and pauses. "When you bathe this evening, please leave your clothes folded on the floor near the door here so they may be tended to."

Tended to?

"And if you get chilled, you will adjust heat here." He taps a circular thermostat on the wall. "Do not exceed seventy-five degrees or there will be consequences."

Consequences? What the actual fuck?

"Okay, wait." I hold up my hands. "Why the hell am I here?"

"To keep you safe."

"See, that's what doesn't make sense. If I'm not safe, don't I have a right to know why? And what's with this consequence bullshit? You're making me sound like a prisoner."

He lets out an impatient breath. "Boss will be by soon to check on you, as will I."

Pissed as I am, I admit to feeling a momentary ripple of excitement at the prospect of seeing my caped savior.

"Does this boss of yours have a name?"

"Yes."

I wait, shrug my shoulders. "Are you going to tell me or do I win the prize if I guess?"

He smirks at me. "Master."

He pulls the door closed and twists the lock.

I don't know how long I stand there staring at the door, willing it to open back up, but I finally feel a chill. I walk to the thermostat and turn it up to 70, then spin around to take in my "accommodations."

The floors are hardwood, polished to a perfect shine. Beautiful, I'll give him that. The room is plenty big enough for one person—probably about 15x15 feet—especially since there's basically no furniture. And no windows. Against the far wall is a thick pillow resting on the floor—dark purple with a dusty rose border that matches the paint on the walls. It looks to be made of velvet, and it's thick. But it looks like nothing more than a dog bed. Big enough for a Great Dane, sure, but a dog bed nonetheless.

I avert my attention to the bathroom, walk inside. A garden tub awaits. So does toilet, single sink, new toothbrush and paste, several bottles of soaps and lotions, and a stack of fuzzy towels and washcloths, all vampire purple. There's also a bottle of ibuprofen and a glass. I fill it up and pop four pills in my mouth, knowing I'll need them.

I walk back out to the room, the heat washing over me. I look at the dog bed and shake my head, decide on a bath. As I step into the tub, I remember my instructions to leave my clothes folded on the floor. Pissed, I get out of the tub, grab my clothes, and leave them where instructed. This time, I push the bathroom door closed until I hear it click and immediately reach for the lock.

That's missing.

Of course.

I roll my eyes and head to the tub, sinking into the warm water. My back is throbbing and my ribs feel tight. The waves tickle my skin, but the warmth feels good. I end up sitting so long that I lose track of time, thinking ... thinking ... thinking ...who would want my demise?

I get out of the water, open the drain. I towel off and pick up a bottle of lotion. It's light pink. I dip my finger in, take a sniff, then wipe it back on the edge of the bottle. When I brush my teeth, my stomach rumbles. I never even had dinner tonight.

I pull the bathroom door open and walk out to the room to turn down the thermostat and get my clothes with every intention of putting them back on, dirty or not. But someone came by and took them while I was bathing. I grumble and twist the knob, but it's locked.

"Are you fucking kidding me?"

I press my ear to the door, hold my breath. All I can hear is the hum of the radiator as it spits out heat. I turn the dial a little to the left, and ticking sounds fill the room as the baseboard coils cool.

And that's it. I have no clothes, no dinner, and nothing but a fucking dog bed to lie on.

You wanted this...

Six months ago~Leigh

Y ou're not too old to put over my knee, you know."

"Do it." I poked his chest. Hard. "I dare you."

Jack snuffed out his cigarette in the ashtray and laughed, pulling me between his legs.

I landed on top of his thigh.

"Maybe one day I will."

"Why wait? One day may never come," I whined, half joking and half serious—but mostly serious—tugging on his shirt and pulling him to me. I rested my forehead on his, staring so deeply into those eyes I was sure I might catch a glimpse of his thoughts.

We had only been dating a month, but the playful banter was always there, hovering over us and egging on our conversations. I liked Jack because he was a smartass and because he seemed to have potential. The kind of potential I needed. Someone who wasn't afraid to rough me up a little. And the reference to the spanking got my motor revving. Except I wasn't sure if it was just a tease.

I was so tired of vanilla men. Any guy can slap your ass when he's doing you from behind. But it takes a special kind of man to turn you over his knee and give it to you good. And I was doing everything in my power to push Jack's buttons so he would do just that.

But he wasn't biting. At least not tonight.

"One day may never come? Always the pessimist, you are."

"I'm not a pessimist. I'm a realist. I see the glass as containing water. Not full and not empty."

"Whatever, crazy." Jack grabbed my breast and twisted my nipple.

I shrieked in pleasure and sucked in a deep breath, hoping for more. Always wanting more. But he put his beer needs ahead of me, reaching across the table to pick up the amber bottle and press it to his lips.

I watched his throat bob up and down as he drank, thinking about all that potential inside of him.

Four

I wake up to something rough scratching my face. My mind is elsewhere in those brief seconds, and I think it's my dad touching me, that I'm back at home and he's still alive. I partially smile before opening my eyes.

And then I see him, the large, towering black shadow hovering over me as I lie on the dog bed.

The caped savior.

And the rough "something" scratching my face is his hand. But his touch is soft—a beautiful dichotomy I don't expect under the circumstances. It's a nice way to awaken in a strange place.

I should be scared, and my heart skips a beat, but I don't lurch off the floor or rush to scoot back against the wall like a frightened animal. I freeze instead, mesmerized by the sheer size of him, and his proximity.

His thumb brushes along my lower lip. It tickles. I wait for him to say something but he's eerily quiet. So quiet I can hear him breathing. I can't see his face but with only a single lamp illuminating the room, it's pretty dark in here.

My stomach rolls with hunger, grumbling like a pissed off bitch. He pauses and twists his head to look over his shoulder, and I see Russia appear holding a tray. Caped savior turns his head to look at me once again, and I search for the fine details of his features.

I push up, holding the towel I had used to cover myself close to my chest. I want to get a better look at him, but I'm relatively certain he's covered his face with a cloth or net because there is nothing but darkness, a blank canvas of nothing. And his hood is up, further obscuring the one part of him I'd really like to see right now.

I know I should be asking a zillion questions, but his presence has me dumbstruck. He sweeps away some of my hair, then lets his fingertips lightly graze down the side of my neck. I feel my skin prickle, my nipples tighten.

He stands up and I follow him with my eyes, letting my gaze flow down his body. The bottom of his cape brushes the floor, just behind his black boots. Fuck, he's huge. He looks at Russia, nods once, and walks out of the room, leaving the door open. I whimper when he's gone.

"I have food for you." Russia kneels, slides the tray along the floor. It's made of bamboo and inlaid with ornate pearl trim and bright colors along the edges. Two bowls rest inside: one a light broth with small vegetables circling the rim and the other a green salad with what looks to be garbanzo beans on top. I smell Italian dressing and it makes my stomach grumble again.

"The soup will help with the pain," he adds.

"Thank you." I pick up the broth and hold it to my nose. "I assume this isn't poisoned."

Russia makes a face. "Don't be ridiculous."

"Had to ask." I look for some utensils but don't see any. "Where's the spoon?"

He stands and crosses his arms. "Utensils must be earned. If you please your Master." So, I'm not being poisoned. Just punished. "In the meantime, we must go over a few things."

"I hope that includes my clothes. Like where they are and when I can get them back?" My heart accelerates, anger rising deep within me. Oddly enough, I don't feel like my life is in danger. But I've been taken hostage—my freedom, my clothes, and the ability to eat with a fucking utensil stripped from me.

"You will wear what your Master wishes you to wear, Leigh. You may keep cover with towels, but you have thermostat to keep warm, and you have soft bed to sleep on. The floor is also heated, so you should not get chilled."

I wrinkle my brow and touch my palm to the floor as he continues.

"There are two rules for now. Rule number one: when your Master enters room, you will sit on floor, on your knees, hands behind back, head lowered. You may use bed if floor hurts your knees. Rule number two: when you speak, you will exercise caution and discipline at all times, addressing him as Master."

Caution?

"I will come by daily to see if you need tending. Are there any questions?"

"Pff," I laugh. "Where do I start? First, how long are you planning, is he planning, to keep me here?"

"As long as it takes."

"As long as what takes?" I pull the towel tighter and tuck it under my arms.

He stares at me for a moment. "Next question?"

I shake my head, exasperated. "Can I at least get a book to read? A candle to burn? Maybe a book or magazine if you have it in your heart?"

"You must earn entertainment."

I drop my head and pinch my nose. This is pointless. Utterly. I wave my hand dismissively. "Great. I'll do that. You can go now."

I glance down at my soup, thinking about hurling it against the wall and starving myself out. But I've never been good at avoiding food.

"Very well. Enjoy your dinner, Leigh."

He closes the door, clicks it locked. I pick up the broth, dip my finger inside to check the heat level. It's warm but not too hot. I lift the bowl to my lips and take a sip. Salty fluid trickles down my throat, blazing a trail of heat that radiates throughout my body. I finish the entire bowl then move to the salad, dropping pieces of lettuce into my mouth, sucking off the salad dressing. Not being able to use a fork is forcing me to eat slower than I'm used to. And in some weird way, it makes it more enjoyable. Which just pisses me off.

When every last piece is gone, I swipe the inside of the bowl and suck the oil and spices from my finger. When I set the bowl back on the tray, I see a small package of crackers. I tear into them and choke them down dry.

With a belly full of food and a small nap on board, my energy is somewhat renewed. I decide to rummage through the drawers in the bathroom. There are only two and they're not very big, but I get excited when I find a bottle of green mud for a face mask. I twist off the top and smear a hefty amount along my skin, constantly brushing my long strands out of the way. I notice a few scratches on my cheek, but they're mostly superficial.

I then plow through the other drawers. I find a pair of tweezers, a pack of travel tissues, a bottle of clear nail polish, an unopened tube of purple lip gloss, a hair tie (I immediately put in my hair), and a block of eyeshadow—tan and pearl. He's either had other chicks here before, or he really planned for me.

I open the sink cabinet and find cleaning products. *Booooooring.*

Oh wait. All the way in the back is a bottle of cheap shampoo/conditioner combo. I'm guessing there isn't a feedback card anywhere around here because I'd be putting my two cents in about this shit right now.

I walk in circles around the room, waiting for my mask to dry. And I do some more thinking about the fucked-up'ness of my situation.

You wanted this…

And I think about the coincidence of it all. How "lucky" I was that the caped savior found me at the exact, precise moment that he did. One minute later and who knows what would have happened. Evil attacker dude could have been shitting on my face. He pretty much had his ass cheeks spread wide over me. And how the hell do they know my name?

But I won't get the answers I need from Russia, and probably not from his boss either. Which leaves only one person: the man who attacked me.

I don't have a crazy ex. Well, I did, but he died several months ago. I work as a vet tech, so I take care of sick and boarding animals all day, assist with surgery, check in clients and take a history, give owners a comforting hug as they say their last goodbyes to their pets. I smile all fucking day long and I cut jokes with my co-workers. I like my boss and I like most of our clients. I haven't had any run-ins with anyone in years. Andrea and I have been best friends since high school, and even *she* hasn't had any recent confrontations I can think of.

But Russia has made it clear I have enemies. Or is that just an excuse to keep me under lock and key? Am I actually going to believe anything he says?

Feeling conflicted, I rub my face, the clay brittle against my fingers. I go to the bathroom and wash it away, then curl up on my bed. I don't bother with a towel because it's warm enough. I run my fingers over my face, smooth like satin. And I think about the caped savior, wondering when I will see him again.

Jack's hands reached up and wrapped around my throat, fingers tightening. I gripped his forearms for balance but I didn't need to. He had me pretty good. I watched as his face curled into a twisted mess of *I'm about to come*. And that disappointed me. I mean, fuck. I had just climbed on top of him. Not only that, it had taken me two months to get him this far.

"I was raised Catholic. I was taught never to hit a woman."

"I'm not asking you to hit me, just be a little rough. Let your beast out."

He had laughed. *"Once I let him out, he may not want to go back in."*

"That's fine. I can handle it."

My face throbbed, my tits bouncing with each slam of his cock. The pulse in my neck thrummed under his fingers.

Jack became fuzzy, everything in the room, fuzzy. My eyes strained in their sockets, things around me going bright and dark all at once. Something tugged at me as Jack's expression wilted away, his face nothing more than the blur of a dream.

I felt this euphoria. It started deep inside of me and it was a wave of recognition, like seeing your twin, or your doppelganger. My body relaxed against the violence being inflicted upon me. I couldn't breathe. My ears hummed. My cunt clenched. My belly tightened.

I was fulfilled for the first time ever.

The tension inside me built, and I felt as though I was about to be gutted. Maybe psychologically I was.

Jack is reaching his potential, I thought, right before losing consciousness.

———

When I woke up, Jack was over me, staring at me with some mild but immeasurable amount of concern.

"You okay?"

I blinked several times. "What happened?"

"Holy shit," he laughed. "You weren't kidding. I let the beast out and it was fucking amazing."

"Jack, you ..." I rubbed my head. It was pounding. "You probably shouldn't let me pass out." I felt weak and dizzy. And a little freaked out.

"You're okay though, right?"

I was okay, if by "okay" he meant hands tingling, body cold and trembling, and skin clammy. Even my mouth was tacky. "I don't know. Can you hold me? Maybe get me some water?"

I needed more than water but didn't know it at the time. He kissed me on the forehead. "Sure, babe. Let me hop in the shower and I'll be right back."

I lay on his bed, trembling like a lost puppy left in a sleet storm. I was so hungry and just wanted a piece of candy or a bowl of ice cream. I felt needy. Why was I so needy all of a sudden?

I couldn't wait for him to get out of the shower. I pushed myself up on the bed and made my way to his kitchen where I cracked open a soda and popped the top to a tube of my favorite chips. And then I went to his couch and laid down where I fell asleep.

I woke up three hours later, uncovered and surrounded by darkness and the melodic *tick-tock* of his grandfather clock.

Five

I hear the *click* but I think it's coming from inside my head, so I don't sit up right away. Just let my eyes stare at the door and struggle to remember where I am and why.

And when I see that long, dark cape flow wide around his feet as he walks in, it all comes rushing back.

Be on your knees, hands behind your back, head bowed, Russia had told me.

I push up and wipe my hair away from my face, thinking what bullshit this all is. I sit on my feet, rest my hands on top of my thighs, and stare at the floor.

He stops six or seven feet from me and my heart drums.

He snaps his fingers. One time. Quick.

I look up at him. Still can't see his face. It's blocked by the hood.

He leans down, taps his hand on his leg.

I push off my legs and start to stand, but he snaps again, then moves his index finger at me in a *no-no* before pointing to the floor.

My jaw clenches. I narrow my eyes and wait.

He taps his leg again, just above the knee, once again summoning me like a fucking pet.

From my dog bed.

Vile liquid crawls up my throat as I get on my hands and knees to crawl to him. My head feels heavy, my eyes bleary, and my body sore and wrecked. I stop in front of him, look at his boots bigger than life, then sit on my feet again. I feel like I'm playing his game without knowing the rules, or what the consequences are if I lose.

He reaches down with one hand, opens his fingers. Rough calluses pepper his palms beneath the knuckles. He wants me to take his hand, so I do, slip my fingers along his. He grips them tight and pulls me up, lifting me with ease.

He's about a foot taller than I am—putting him at about six and a half feet, give or take. I point my gaze at him, but as soon as I'm standing, he swiftly moves behind me, pressing his hands to my shoulders and creating a current of air that swirls around me. He smells like earth and spice, like something dark yet peaceful.

The backs of his hands run down my arms, slowly, until he gets to my wrists. My nipples pucker, which has me questioning everything about this situation, and about me.

I expect his hands to keep wandering, move to my stomach or the many other parts of me that are exposed right now. There must be a reason he wants me naked, and I don't think it takes a rocket scientist to figure out what that reason is.

But instead of exploring me, his hands brush my hair over my shoulder before securing a metal band around my neck. It's cold against my skin. Something clicks into place, and I hear chains rattling behind me. I turn my head to look, but he presses two fingers to my cheek, forcing me to face the door again.

He fastens something to the band on my neck, then walks ahead of me, a silver leash flowing over his shoulder as he pulls me along. Instant panic ices me but I have no choice but to walk, to follow the caped savior, my master.

The air feels chilly as we step into the hall. My skin pimples and fear floods me as I face the uncertainty of where we're going. I listen to his boots shuffle along the floor. His cape brushes against my shins as he walks. His strides are long—two of my steps to his one.

We wind around the corner, pass the foyer and turn, stopping in front of a large wooden door. I reach up to touch the band around my neck as he twists the handle and opens the door. I can feel the circle of the O-ring and the metal clasp attached to the leash. It connects me to him, for however long he wishes to leave it in place.

Sunlight slices through the air, making me squint. I expect cold air to punch me as we step onto a porch, but tall bronze lamps rest at both corners, radiating heat around us. Reaching to our left, he pulls a thick fur coat off a rack and snakes behind me, wrapping it around my shoulders. It feels nearly hot against my skin. He then leads me through the porch door and into the open air where the sun warms my face and makes me feel like maybe there is hope.

He turns me until I'm facing south, the sunrise low and blinding me, then undoes the leash. And although I'm squinting painfully, I still try to steal a glimpse of his face. But it doesn't do any good. He walks away, back to the porch where he crosses his arms over his chest and watches me.

I pull the fur coat tight and feel a shudder as I glare at him, wondering what he wants me to do, why he's left me here. I'm surrounded by dozens of rose bushes, all dead of course since it's November. A trail of red and yellow pansies line the border of the rose garden. A black metal fence, topped with alternating spokes and bats and standing at least seven feet tall, will keep me from escaping, if I were to think about it.

"What do you want from me?" I ask.

His silence hits me hard. He takes a step back, into the shadows of the porch. I release a long breath and shake my head, spinning around to look at the garden. Maybe there's a clue around here, like a hidden, super-secret message. But the grass is too cold and scratchy to wander very far without shoes.

I decide to sit on the ground, lie down and shimmy my feet up to my butt. I pull the bottom of the coat over them, covering my toes with fur. I close my eyes and let my time in the sun pass in silence.

When I hear the double beep of a digital watch, I turn my head in his direction, watching as he swings the door open and approaches me, extending a hand to help me up.

He lifts me off the ground, attaches the leash, and leads me inside after removing my coat and placing it on the hook. I've had no more than five minutes of fresh air, but I'm so hungry and jonesing for coffee that I don't mind going back in.

He walks me to my room, all the way to the dog bed, and snaps his finger before pointing to the floor. I don't have to guess. He wants me kneeling again. So down I go, lowering myself until all I see is floor and boots.

I look up at his figure towering above me as he unclips the leash. "Do you treat all your guests like this or am I special?"

He holds still for a second, then his hand comes flying at my face. I'm sure he's about to slap me, but instead, he grips it so tightly, my teeth dig into the insides of my cheeks. My heart hammers, fear rippling through my veins. I can hear his anger pulsing out with each breath he takes. Then he releases me and stands upright. His cape opens wide as his hand comes out and balls into a fist. He lifts it and punches the wall, rattling everything in the room.

Stunned, I jerk back, keep my eyes down. And I feel a flurry of emotions when I hear his boots shuffling, the door closing, the click of the lock.

I touch the collar on my neck, holding my fingers against the cold steel for several minutes, wondering what I said to set him off. It sure doesn't seem to take much. And frankly, I'm surprised that I have that much power over him, to cause him to explode like that.

When I hear the door opening minutes later, I assume he's coming back to apologize. But it's Russia who appears. He stands in front of me then squats to my level.

"Are you all right, Leigh?"

His question lacks the inflection at the end, like it's not a real question. As if he knows, like he could hear the punch on the wall. As though he can see the layers and layers of emotions I'm experiencing right now.

"You tell me. You know more about my future than I do."

He pulls in a long breath. "I tried to make clear that your master expects you to address him as such, and that he demands respect at all times. You've learned a lesson that has cost no more than pride at this point."

My stomach rolls. At this point? So, there are more glorious occasions to look forward to, more lessons to learn that might cost me more?

You wanted this...

"It's no matter now. Your master requests your presence at the breakfast table. Please remember the rules as I have instructed of you."

I look up at him, wondering if I'm supposed to stand or if I have to wait for further instructions.

"You may follow me. Your master is the only one who uses leash."

This is some fucked up bullshit. I guess I should be grateful I'm being fed, but I'm not looking forward to sitting at a table with a stranger who won't talk to me.

And on the way to breakfast, I'm informed of yet another rule.

"Your master's face is exposed so he may eat. When we arrive to the breakfast table, you will keep your gaze to the floor at all times. Understood?"

"Yes."

I keep my gaze down the whole way there, and when Russia pushes open a door, I hear the sounds of plates clinking, feet shuffling. A large, white cloth snaps in the air and falls to the floor. I can barely see out of the corner of my eye, but caped savior is there, facing me, no doubt making sure I'm following the rules.

My palms dampen. My chest hums. My stomach ripples. The urge to look at him is so powerful it's about to win. But, somehow, I know that punch to the wall was just a sampling of what this man can do. I don't know that I fear him, but I do have a newfound respect for him, small as it is.

"I will return for you when your meal is finished."

Russian disappears, and several pairs of feet scurry out of the room. I'm alone with him.

I can see that he's sitting at the head of the table. And then he snaps his fingers, points to the white cloth next to the legs of the table, where I guess I'm supposed to sit and eat.

I can feel my blood pressure rise, insulted that he expects me to sit on the floor. Newfound respect, gone. Part of me wants to stand my ground, to stay put, dig my heels in. But when he snaps his finger again and points, I know I better move.

Like an obedient prisoner, I sit on my knees as expected and wonder if he's going to throw scraps of food down at me. But the moment my knees hit the floor, a door opens to my right and someone carries in a tray of food, setting it down in front of me. Eggs, turkey bacon, a buttered English muffin and some blueberries are what I have to enjoy. A steaming cup of coffee sits next to a tall glass of orange juice. My mouth waters. And still no silverware. But I don't even care.

Using my fingers, I finish every bite. My eating is sloppy and loud as I suck crumbs off my fingers and gulp down the whole glass of juice at once. His eating, however, is quiet. Even the way he uses his utensils seems controlled. Maybe he eats with his fingers, too. I find myself wanting to burst into laughter, that ball of desire building up deep within me. I bite my lip and hold it back, pulling the cup of coffee to my mouth, pressing the rim of the mug to my lips, and letting the bitter black substance move down my throat.

When I'm finished, the awkwardness of the silence is thick. I wish he'd talk to me. I don't even care what he says. Just say something for fuck's sake. My legs fall asleep so I pull them out from underneath me and press the soles of my feet together. I glance between my legs, noticing the stubble already forming there. Well, I know what I'll be doing today, if I can find a razor, that is. I didn't think to look last night.

He pushes his chair out and stands, walks to me, extends a hand. I know the drill by now. He pulls a leash out from somewhere ... I don't know, thin air?... clips it to my collar, leads me down the hall. I flick my gaze up at his back, noticing he has dark hair, but I'm afraid of staring.

He doesn't take me to my room. Instead, we end up somewhere else. It's hard to tell since I can't look up, but I definitely hear a fire crackling, feel the heat. I see the bottom of a long shelf and what appears to be dozens of books, but it's not the same room I passed through yesterday when I arrived. It smells earthy in here and not just from the fire. It smells of leather and paper. And history.

He walks to a couch and turns to face me. It would be so easy to look at him right now. Almost worth a slap to the face.

Once my leash is unclipped, he sits, the leather squeaking under his weight.

In my periphery, I catch him looking at me, his head angling upward, his eyes piercing me. I think I feel something from him, too. Maybe disapproval, maybe mere curiosity. Or maybe I'm reading too much into it.

I take a step back. He does the *snap-point* thing again, this time right at his feet and those big, black boots. I go down, feeling wobbly. But beneath me is a thick oriental rug that feels good on my legs and butt. The heat from the fire wraps around my body.

I stare at the rug, noticing the diamond pattern and the green and gold and orange flecks woven into the fabric. From the corner of my eyes, I watch his hands travel smoothly up and down the tops of his dark slacks.

Then he reaches over, runs his fingers through my hair. He presses the side of my head until it's resting on his knee and he caresses me. I feel his nails gently graze my scalp, and then his hand starts to flow to my shoulder. My skin tingles. My body relaxes like putty. I don't know what to think.

He pulls in a deep breath, and when he exhales, a soft growl escapes. I hear his lips part, as if he's about to tell me something. But then Russia walks in the room.

"Boss, sorry to interrupt, but he's here now."

I feel his body shake and see a quick hand wave before Russia disappears.

His fingertips slide around my neck, down my clavicle to the top of my breast. I stiffen, wondering if he will take it further, and if I will let him. But he doesn't. He only lets his fingertips brush up and down my skin nearby, forcing my nipples to tingle.

And then he stops, brushes my hair aside and gently pushes me off his knee. After standing up, he reaches for my hand and lifts me, fastening the leash and leading me out of the library.

I'm taken back to my room, but he walks behind me to unfasten my leash. His hand brushes down the side of my arm before he walks away. And the last thing I'm left with is the sound of the door closing and locking, and my heart beating in my ears.

I want to try something with you." Jack was holding a black leather handle with long tendrils extending down, all of them knotted at the end.

"What the hell is that?" I asked.

"It's called a cat o' nine tails. I've been doing some research, and apparently this bad boy delivers a powerful punch."

I stared at the whip, touching the dark straps that danced in the air as he held it out for me. I shouldn't have been surprised that he wanted to take it to the next level. I had sort of created this monster.

"This looks like it would hurt," I said, rolling one of the knots between my fingers.

I said I liked it rough. Not that I wanted to be whipped to a bloody pulp.

An evil smile spread across his face. Jesus, I really *had* created a monster.

"That's the plan. I think you would like it, Leigh. I've been reading up on this S&M stuff. And I think this is what's been missing from your life. From *our* lives."

Jack and I openly admitted that we had struggled in our previous relationships, constantly dealing with issues of incompatibility, especially in the bedroom. I knew I had a side with darker needs. But experiencing physical pain had never been something that enticed me.

Still, I was somewhat curious. And I'd be lying if I didn't admit that the thought of being punished while helplessly restrained to a bedpost did excite me a little.

"Go easy on me?" I told him, posed more as a question because I wasn't sure if he knew how to do that.

Jack had shown me fairly quickly just how rough he could get. And he was a little on the careless side. Dig one butt plug out of me, shame on you. Dig two, shame on me. Needless to say, Jack had only gone on one butt-plug diving adventure up my rectum. I'd made him use a ripcord after that. But still, I was getting more and more concerned that he didn't know what he was doing.

"Of course I'll go easy on you," he said, setting the whip down and cupping my face.

For whatever reason, I felt reassured by his promise. And before I knew it, I was on his bed, ass up and face down as he began striking me.

At first, his blows were soft, almost tickling my flesh. But he quickly advanced to a harder strike, the tendrils burning like hundreds of fire ants. I gripped the comforter, my body jerking with each hit.

"Fuck, baby, your ass is turning a hot shade of red. So fucking sexy..."

Knowing that Jack was turned on made me want to continue. I wanted to be able to handle whatever he dished out. But then he upped the ante, and I could hear the leather lashes whistling in the air as he brought the cat o' nine tails down on me. The knots punched my flesh like the knuckles of a fist. I cried out, partly in pain, but also from the rush at the intensity of the blows.

Jack didn't stop. But I didn't tell him to. I wanted to keep going, see how far I could be pushed.

I could learn to enjoy this.

Jack was the first person I'd been with who was willing to explore these things with me. Willing to push the envelope and live up to that potential I knew he had.

I don't know how long Jack hit me, but when I finally told him *I can't*, he joined me, pressing his naked body against mine and pushing his erection deep inside of me. He held my legs open and drove himself in and out, telling me how wet I was. His chest rubbed against my back, and his harsh movements irritated my already inflamed skin.

And I couldn't even look him in the eye to communicate to him how lost I felt in that moment.

I tried to come but couldn't. I felt sick inside, lying to myself about how deeply connected to Jack I felt because of what I had allowed him to do. But the truth was, I didn't feel connected to him at all.

I felt disconnected. To him and to myself.

And the disconnect only worsened when he pulled out of me, gave me a quick kiss on the cheek, and left me to take a shower. I cried then, and I cried over the next two days, angry at myself and angry at him. I called out sick because I felt like I had the flu. I took five hot baths and drank tea and ate lollipops like they were the new drug of choice.

I thought about breaking up with Jack. Obviously, this wasn't working. And it's not like I was in love with him. Neither of us had dropped the "L" word. So when he called me three days after the whipping, I told him we needed to talk. He said that he agreed and that I should come to his house.

I assumed he wanted to end things with me, too. I never would have guessed what he really wanted.

Six

I sit huddled on my bed. I've been here about twelve hours and already been stripped, fed, and cuddled by my captor.

The biggest thing I miss right now are my clothes. It's weird how we take these "automatics" in our lives for granted. I would settle for a simple pair of underwear. There's something uncomfortable about this constant dampness between your legs, rubbing along your thighs. It's a feeling of vulnerability that's hard to describe.

I lie down on my bed and stare at the painting on the ceiling. And I think about that dampness and where it's coming from. I close my eyes and feel his fingers on me again, tickling my neck, trailing down to my breast. I imagine him moving lower, teasing my nipples, getting me wetter.

And then I think about watching him punch the wall, the way his body seemed to move like a pendulum as his arm rose high preparing to strike, then swayed to the side after his fist came down.

As I lie here, I imagine my slender body writhing under his enormous frame. I picture him punching shit, damaging things, slapping me and drilling me with his giant cock. I wonder why he wears that fucking cape and realize it's that exact mystery that turns me on.

My insides ache with desire. I run a hand up my body, touching my breasts and wrapping my fingers around my neck, just below the collar. I part my lips and dip a finger inside my slit, coming out to circle my clit. I huff and draw my legs up. My pulse races as I try to put a face to the man who holds me here.

When I hear the click of the door, I throw my legs back down and sit up, tucking my hair behind my ears right as Russia makes an appearance.

"Your presence is requested outside. Please follow me."

My nipples are still puckered tight, and the thought of going back outside in the cold doesn't help matters. But if Russia notices my arousal, he doesn't give any indication.

I follow him down the hall and to the back porch. I feel the blast of cool air when the door is opened. And I hear the cries of a pleading man as Russia passes the fur coat to me. Ignoring him, I step closer to the porch door, pressing my fingers to the screen and peering out. Two men wearing wool coats are restraining another man, pulling his arms behind his back and lifting him off the ground. His sandy blond hair looks disheveled, and large bruise decorates his left eye. He kind of resembles a traumatized ballerina right now, his tippy-toes dancing along the ground as he trembles and whimpers.

"I won't do anything again. I promise. You can trust me," he says, eyes wide, voice high and fevered.

That voice. I recognize it right away.

Caped savior stands with arms crossed, his cape and hood covering him once again from head to toe.

I feel the fur coat being draped over my shoulders and Russia pushes the door open, guiding me outside as he asks, "Do you have anything you'd like to say to your attacker, Leigh?"

I look his way, then to Savior. Both are watching me.

I swallow hard, a thick lump in my throat, thinking this is why I've been held here. That once I have the chance to speak my mind, I'll be let go, and they will deal with the man who attacked me. That's why his face is covered. Because he doesn't want me to be able to identify him. And maybe Russia will go back to his home country.

"Why did you do it?"

His laugh is sickly, as if to say it was all just a big misunderstanding. He looks at Savior, almost as if he's asking for permission. He shakes his head in a slow back-and-forth warning.

"I want to tell you," he whimpers. "But ..." He pauses, looks to the ground.

Savior takes a step closer, walking behind the three men. His hood points up high, his height dwarfing them.

"But what?" I ask, trying to get a read on him. I should be afraid, scared to be in his presence. "Why did you attack me?" I pull the coat tighter, flick my gaze up at my rescuer towering behind him. I swear he's staring right at me. I know he is. I see the blink of his eyes and feel the rush of excitement rippling right through to my core.

But then I shiver as my attacker looks back up to me, snarling and licking his lips. "They won't let me," he grumbles. "I wanted to tell you everything about it, about how—"

He doesn't get a chance to finish. Savior fists his hair, yanks his head back, and slides a knife across his throat. His body flails momentarily as the guards tighten their grip. Garbled choking sounds come from his mouth as a river of blood pours down the front of him, streams of red spurting from his neck with every beat of his heart.

My mouth falls open in disbelief, just in time for Russia to cup my elbow and lead me away. My breath quickens, and I twist my head around to look at the scene once again. My attacker's lifeless body slumps to the cold earth. I hear it *thump*. Savior takes a step back and lifts his head to watch me as I'm led away.

He gives me one nod. One affirmation.

And I think I know what he's telling me.

That he avenged my attack for me.

That he has rightfully earned the title of *Master*.

I'm shaking as I'm led back to my room. And I stumble to my bed where I fall down.

Russia stands over me for a moment before kneeling. "Your master wishes to make it clear that no one will ever try to harm you again. He'll see to it."

I stare at him, empty of words for the first time since I got here. With all the unanswered questions on top of what I just witnessed, my mind is a swirling vortex of emotions and thoughts that I couldn't possibly put in some semblance of order, even if I wanted to. But I'd be lying if I didn't admit that I feel a hint of excitement that someone is willing to protect me to that level.

I just wish I knew why.

He stands to leave but I stop him.

"What's your name?" I don't know why suddenly this is important. But maybe I need to feel more connected to someone here. Plus, I'm really tired of thinking of him as a country.

He looks over his shoulder at me, then answers. "Victor."

"Victor," I repeat. "Is that Russian?"

He turns to look at me, smirks. "Yes. But I am Romanian."

I nod. "Thank you, Victor."

"I will see you soon, Leigh."

After he leaves, I expect my savior to come to me. But I don't know what I would do if I saw him walk in here right now. I hug myself and let the images that have been burned in my mind flash once again.

What would possess him to do something like that? And what would make him think I would want to see it? Does he think that will bring me some sense of closure? *Does* it bring me closure?

Too anxious to sit around, I draw myself a bath. On the corner of the tub is a small box of pink oil-filled pearls and a pink bottle. On the front is a picture of a smiling, pink bubble surrounded by dozens of smaller blue bubbles. I used to have this same bottle as a kid. I pick it up and twist the lid, put it to my nose, and pull in the scent.

They say that sense of smell is more deeply connected to our memories than any other sense, and in this case, it's true. My memories slam into me: the house I grew up in, my dad bathing me on Saturday nights before his friends would come over to play poker, tying my hair up in pigtails before school, making my lunches and walking me to the bus stop, kissing me on the cheek. And, my dad always made sure I had my bubbles.

I hug the bottle to my chest for just a moment, remembering, wishing, aching, sinking. Sorrow is so heavy. I shake the memories away because if I let them stay too long they'll consume me.

I pour in a hefty amount of liquid. Within five minutes, bubbles are climbing the tile walls. I get in the tub, hearing them *snap* and *pop* as I sit. I mindlessly poke at them, then flatten my palm and sink it into the bubbles, feeling them fizzle around my fingers. I scoop some up and cover my cheeks like shaving cream, remembering that's what daddy did.

"And one dollop on the nose for good measure," he'd say, leaning so close I could smell the tobacco on his breath.

I would giggle and ask him to do it again.

"Tomorrow," he'd answer.

I lean back in the tub and close my eyes. The water is so warm I can't help but fall asleep. But when I wake up, it's cool. I shiver as my eyes open. Then I pull in a hard breath because I see he's there, leaning against the door frame, his arms crossed as he watches me. A light purple towel provides a stark contrast to his black cape as it rests draped across his shoulder.

I bolt upright and mutter a *Jesus* under my breath before realizing that probably isn't showing him the respect he wants. And then I start to apologize, but I figure it's too late. So I turn my head away and cast my gaze at the water. All the bubbles are gone, except for a few floating on the slick surface of the water.

After ten or so seconds, I realize how awkward this is. Is he just going to stand there and stare at me? Or is he actually waiting for me to say something? All I can hear are the sounds of my breathing. My pulse pounds. In my mind, I see the man falling to the ground again. I swallow and look his way, keeping my eyes pointed at his feet.

"I ... I don't know what you want from me. Master."

The last word barely slips from my lips. It comes out so quietly I'm not even sure he can hear me. I don't like the way it feels coming out of me. I don't like the way it sounds. I'm not a genie and I'm not a fucking slave.

He pushes off the wall and walks to me, those big boots *thump-thump-thumping* along the linoleum. He pulls the towel off his shoulder and lets it drop in the air, then holds it open for me to step into. I push down the drain and stand up. Then I hold up my arms so he can wrap the towel around me. But he doesn't wrap the towel around me. Instead, he starts patting my arms dry, first one then the other, all the way to my fingers.

Then he brushes the cotton over my front, wiping my chest and belly and gently dabbing my breasts. My body tingles, responding in a way I wish it wouldn't, at least with him. It takes every ounce of will power I have *not* to look up at him, even with the black hood covering his face.

He steps back and curls two fingers quickly and I step onto the rug. He spins one finger in the air for me to turn around, so I do. And he proceeds to dry my backside, going all the way down my thighs, my knees, and to my calves, pressing his hands into my flesh along the way. I hold back a groan as the dampness between my legs returns.

He rises, and out of the corner of my eye, I watch him neatly fold the towel before hanging it on the bar to dry. He fumbles with something for a few moments, then places a finger on my chin and gently nudges me back around.

He clips a leash to my collar, this one long and thin and made of leather. He then brushes his thumb along my cheek. I hear him exhale, dark and deep and almost rumbly, as if he wants to growl. My body tenses because I'm sure he's getting ready to say something.

But he spins on his feet and starts walking, the leash falling down the back of his shoulder and connecting to me as he leads me out of my room. When we get to the end of the hall this time, he turns left, bringing us to a narrow winding staircase. The metal is cold on my feet as we climb up, and I have to hold on to the railing because the stairs are so steep.

Once we reach the top, he takes me down another hallway and into a room that's fit for royalty. A four-poster king-size bed rests against the far wall, its wood carved, dark, and brooding. The comforter is thick and spills forth earthy tones of orange and brown. Golden fibers glint from the small amount of light trickling through the triangular stained-glass window. Two bedside tables each hold a multi-tiered, tree-shaped candelabra, their gnarled, golden branches dripping frozen wax and twisting in an erotic display of life and chaos.

He casts me a look over his shoulder as I stare, mesmerized. Then he flicks his head and leads me to a door at the other end of the room. When he opens it, it's like my very own surprise awaits. A walk-in closet with shirts, blouses, dresses, slacks, jeans, slutty clothes, business clothes, boots, sandals, heels, and every style you could ever imagine waits for me over a double expanse of twenty feet.

"I can have these?"

He doesn't answer. No shock there.

I look his way, without glancing at his face, and he holds up three fingers.

"Three things?" I ask.

Damn. Okay. I can work with this. Obviously, I need a top and bottom, so I'll start there. The first thing that catches my attention is a sleeveless, backless, multi-colored blouse that was made for clubbing. I pull it off the bar, running my fingers over it. I'd look sexy as fuck in this.

But, I know it's not very practical. I should be going for comfort, right? Following that logic, I know my room is warm and I'll get the coat when I go outside. So, letting out a sigh of disappointment, I flip through the clothes, settling on some tight black leggings for pants. They'll be comfortable for sleeping in. Next, I choose a bright yellow sleeveless V-neck shirt. Yellow because it's supposed to be a happy color, and I've never owned anything yellow. Don't know why because as I hold it to my arm, it seems to be perfect against my skin tone.

I take a step back and check out the shoes, leaning down to pick up a pair of sneakers. They all look brand new, and I can't imagine why they're all here. And why they all look to be my size. I start to try them on, but he reaches over and takes the shoes from my hands before dropping them to the floor. He pushes several items of clothes out of the way and removes the cool blouse I was looking at moments ago. And then he passes it to me. I guess this is the third item he wants me to have.

He flicks his head again and leads me out of the closet, pushing the door closed before walking me out of the room. My insides twist and fall because I really want to stay here, look out the window some, enjoy a room with a bed, with golden trees that have gnarled branches and a closet full of clothes. At least in here, being alone wouldn't seem all that bad.

On the way back to my room, we pass Victor in the hallway. Savior stops him, unclasps my leash, and taps him on the shoulder.

Victor nods.

And then he's gone, walking down the long hallway and turning the corner. I watch his shadow twist and elongate on the wall and across the floor after he's out of sight.

Victor brings me back to my room. Next to the bathroom door now is a small three-tiered shelf that someone must have just put in here. On the top sits a single orchid in a miniature vase of water. Its satin white outer petals darken to an inner fleshy pink, the smaller petals inside resembling a vulva, swollen with desire.

"You may put your clothes there. Lunch will be served soon."

"Did you do this?"

"I brought in shelves. I did not pick flower."

He starts to pull the door closed when I stop him.

"Victor? Please, leave the door unlocked. I won't try to leave."

It's actually the truth. I'm officially afraid of what's out there.

"The lock is not to keep you in."

I pull back. "What's it for then?"

"To keep them out."

And then he is gone, twisting the lock.

I kneel on the floor and look at the orchid, sensing this is more than my savior wanting to pretty up my space. I feel this is a message. A very erotic message. My stomach flutters. But the flutters twist in on themselves and die when I realize this has to be some sort of fucked up trap.

Four months ago~Leigh

I sat on the couch in Jack's apartment, my gut churning. He lit a cigarette and asked me if I wanted a glass of Merlot.

"You have Merlot?"

"I bought some just for you. You want a glass?"

I shook my head. If he was offering me wine, he didn't plan to break up with me, unless he bought it out of guilt.

"You mind if I have a beer?" he asked.

"When have I ever cared that you drank a beer?"

"I just want to be sure. I've got some heavy shit to talk with you about. Maybe I ought to be sober."

I lifted an eyebrow in question. This was not sitting well with me.

He sucked on his Marlboro and sat on the sofa, twisting to face me. "Look. I know things have been off between us lately. I know that's what you came here to talk about."

"Honestly, I didn't come here to exactly talk."

He ran his fingers through his hair. "I figured as much. I know you prefer sex to talking a lot of the time. But I really think we need to open the door to communication here."

Jesus, is that what he thought? That I came here to fuck? I thought back to the conversation we had a few hours ago. The one where I told him we needed to *talk*. He was making assumptions again. Assumptions that I wanted the same things he did.

He was right about one thing though; we had some catching up to do in the communication department.

"Look, Jack. I need to say some things that you don't want to hear."

"You don't like what I've been doing to you in the bedroom. I know."

"You... you do?" I pulled back.

"Yes. At first, I thought that maybe you were surprised I had it in me. But we've been together long enough now that you shouldn't be shocked by my roughness."

Hmm. A few months is hardly long enough to *really* know someone. To know what they're capable of. You may think, but you don't know.

"And I have to admit, I got a little frustrated with you because you said that's what you wanted. Someone to rough you up. But I got to thinking." He tugged on his smoke, and white clouds streamed out of his nostrils as he stomped it out in the ashtray. "Maybe I'm roughing you up the wrong way."

His words jarred me. It wasn't the roughness I didn't like. It was ... what was it? I couldn't put my finger on it. I guess he had nailed it. We were just ... off.

"Jack, I don't know where you're going with this, but-"

"Just hear me out, babe." He brushed some hair out of my face.

I felt impatient, like bugs were crawling on my skin and I needed to run outside and spray myself down with the garden hose.

"Okay," I relented, scratching at my arms.

He took me by the hand, a rarity for Jack, and danced those blue eyes of his around my face. I never was very good at resisting his good looks. "I want you to think about how we've been doing things since I unleashed my inner beast. Everything that I've done to you has been … tactile. I squeeze your neck. I pull your hair. I twist your nipples until you scream. I lash you with the cat. All hands-on, right?"

"Yes. Pretty much." Nothing complicated there.

"Right," he said, pausing. "But now, I want you to imagine things being different. Try to imagine what it would be like if I could bring you into that same head space without even touching you?"

I stared at him, waiting for an explanation. It seemed like he was being overly mysterious. Dramatic. Tour de force.

"I don't see how that's possible."

"It is, Leigh. It's very possible." He leaned forward and cupped my face, pulling me so close I could almost taste the sweetness of his cigarette. "It's called *mindfuck*."

Seven

When I hear the click of my door, I can hardly jump up fast enough. But as soon as I see who it is, I lower myself back to the floor, grabbing my collar instinctively as I settle on my knees and lower my gaze. I won't put my arms behind my back. I refuse to take this shit to that level. I guess when it comes to following orders, I excel at half-assing it.

He puts his hand under my arm and pulls me up, then places the leash on the O-ring. The backs of his fingers flow down the front of my blouse—the one he selected for me—passing right between my breasts. I study his hand, noticing how rough it looks, how the deep ridges ingrained in his flesh show years of hard work, of fighting. His knuckles look so large I know there's power in his grip.

He slips a finger through the slit between the first and second buttons, running the top of his nail along my flesh. My insides tremble. My breath quickens. I think I feel him smile. Maybe it's the sound of his breathing. It seems to have changed, lightened. I still hold the image of him slitting my attacker's throat, yet his touch is like an instant eraser to that vision. And it's also a bringing me to a place I haven't been in a while. I feel the heat between my legs.

He grips the top button and slides it through the hole, then does the same for the next one down. And the next one, and the next one. My pulse races as he opens my blouse and exposes me to him. Even though he's already seen me, it feels like this is the first time.

Lifting the leash, he touches the metal chain to my nipple, first one and then the other. The cold bites my flesh and I feel my skin tighten, curl into a point.

He wraps the chain around my neck several times, letting the handle dangle over the back of my shoulder. He cups my breasts, sweeps his thumbs over the points of my nipples, still tingling from the bite of the leash. Warmth surges through me and I feel betrayed by my own body. It's nothing more than traitorous to want his touch. And then, just like that, he buttons me back up.

After gathering my leash, he leads me to the kitchen where my white floor tablecloth awaits. He points down as we approach the table, as if there is any confusion about where I'm to sit. Feeling like a pro after only two meals out here, I sit down and wait for my dinner. This time, however, I sit facing him and even though I'm not looking up at him, I can still see when he pulls the hood off. It would be so easy to steal a glance, to take a quick peek in the hopes that he won't see. But I'm not feeling that ballsy yet.

To my left, I see four feet approaching. My gaze travels up quickly, and I can see that two women, completely unclothed except for their collars, are carrying plates our way. One of them walks to me, the other, to him. I take my plate and glass from her.

Tonight's course is baked salmon with whole potatoes and chargrilled asparagus.

My mouth waters.

I stare at the two sets of feet on either side of him, their nails plain and unpainted but clean. Above, I notice they're practically hovering over him, waiting on him hand and foot. And it's like this through the entirety of our meal. The silence is driving me nuts.

"May I get you anything else, Master?"

Finally.

Wait, what?

My stomach tenses at the way she addresses him.

There's a hierarchy here, and I'm at the bottom of the totem pole.

He doesn't say anything to her, but I think he gestures something. I can only see brief movement from the corner of my eye.

"Very well, Master." A pause. "It would be an honor to sleep in your bed tonight, Master. Please consider choosing me as your evening companion."

My eyes swell to the size of saucers.

"Master," the other one says, her voice high and squeaky. "It would be an honor sleeping in your bed tonight. Please consider choosing *me* as your companion."

I don't know what happens, what choice he makes, because my heart is beating so fast it's pulsing the blood through my veins, making it roar in my ears. I see him again, standing behind my attacker and slitting his throat, forcing blood to shoot out like ejaculate from his neck.

What if I've been taken prisoner for his harem?

"Thank you, Master," one of the women responds. "I'm honored you have chosen me. I will prepare myself to your liking."

I throw a hand over my mouth, feeling my dinner churn in my stomach, rise in my throat. I take a deep breath and swallow it down, lifting my glass of water and finishing what's left.

I watch their feet walk away, feel the tension mount as we're alone again.

This is the first time I don't want to look at him, that my curiosity is buried under a mountain of anger. But dinner is over, so I have to let him clip the leash around my neck and wonder how much longer I will have to do this.

How much longer I will be forced to eat on the floor with my hands.

How much longer I will be forced to live in silence and call him Master.

How much longer I will be forced to endure his presence without knowing my place in his life.

Why I am here.

The library is the last place I want to go with him, but that's where he takes me. To the same spot and with the same commands—snapping, pointing. He pulls my head to his knee again, stroking my hair. Someone comes in, brings him a drink, sets it on the table. I hear the ice cubes clinking the edge of the glass, hear him swallow, feel his nails graze along the flesh of my shoulder.

Feel myself fall victim to his touch.

I stare at his boots, my body melting involuntarily against his.

He's going to sleep with another woman tonight. She knows what he looks like, what he sounds like. What he fucks like.

Why can't he just say one thing to me?

"Master?" I ask. Now I officially hate that word. "Can I ask you a question?"

I turn my head in his direction, being careful to avoid looking up at him, when we're interrupted.

"A moment of your time, please, Master?" It's one of the girls from dinner. The one with the high, squeaky voice.

I look in her directions. She stands naked in the doorway, arms at her sides. She flashes me a caustic look.

"I have been loyal to you for all these months, nearly a year."

She steps inside the room, and his hand freezes on my shoulder.

"And I have been waiting patiently for you to allow me the honor of joining you in bed. Yet you consistently deny me, turn me away. For *her*."

His breath pulls in, tight as ever. His grip tightens on my shoulder and I can feel the tension oozing from him. The anger, sharp and deep.

"I need to know, Master, why? Why am I here if not to serve you in *every* way?"

Jesus. I don't know whether to feel revolted or embarrassed for her. I guess it's a mixture of both.

He stands and walks to her, his hands in fists at his side. I see his head, covered in dark, wavy hair. His walk is slow. She keeps her eyes pointed at him as he approaches her, and I wonder why she's allowed to look at him and I'm not.

My heart pounds as he stops in front of her. She has to crane her neck just to make eye contact with him. Her small breasts swoop down and point to him as he lifts a hand, places it around her throat, and tilts his head. He then presses her back into the wall. She coughs, grabs his forearm and struggles to get free as her feet kick wildly around his shins.

"Please…" she chokes. "Master…"

I stare helplessly at the scene, watching as this girl's face blooms red. She sticks her tongue out, struggling to breathe when Victor walks in.

"Boss!" he snaps.

Savior lowers her to the floor and releases her. She throws her hands to her throat and sucks in some air, her upper body heaving.

Victor moves between them, pulling the girl by her wrist while staring at my savior in shock. Like he's never seen him do anything like that before.

"You will collect your things and leave immediately," Victor tells her.

"Yeah," she sputters. "No shit, I will. Should have done that a long time ago."

She barges past him and runs out the door. Victor places his hand on Savior's shoulder, looks at him with concern. His back is still to me, but I can see his shoulders rising and falling with every deep breath. He rolls his head in a circle, and Victor flashes me a quick look.

I realize I'm trembling, my fingernails digging into the flesh of my thighs. But not because I'm scared. I'm ... I'm...?

"You wish for me to take her back?" Victor asks, tilting his head in my direction.

Savior nods, then brushes past Victor and walks out of the room. I watch him until he's out of sight, a part of me wishing he'd turn and look at me.

So, they just let that girl go willingly? I don't know what to make of that. But clearly, not everyone is here against their will.

When I get back to my room, Victor closes the door behind him and moves close to me.

"Are you okay?"

I laugh and shake my head. "Am I the one who needs checking on or the girl who was almost choked to unconsciousness?"

"Don't be disturbed by what you saw. She has been trouble from beginning. Not like you."

"I can be trouble, Victor. Believe me," I say, crossing my arms and narrowing my eyes. "What the hell kind of organization are you all running here? Why is she allowed to leave but not me, huh?" My anger escalates with my voice as I continue, my fists clenching as I feel my fury reaching an all-time high. "You want noise, I'll give you noise. I'll give you all the noise it takes for him to come in here, smash me against a wall, and slit my throat, too. That'll leave you with one hell of a mess to clean up."

I huff as Victor holds up both hands and glances at the door. I hope he *does* come in. I would fucking welcome it.

"Okay, fine. Please, calm down. I will explain."

"I want answers now. Or I'm going to scream until someone shuts me up."

"Fine," he snaps, increasingly agitated. "I said I will explain. Just give me a moment."

He runs his hands through his hair and paces the floor.

Feeling like I've achieved a small victory, I sit on my bed and lean against the wall.

"There are certain things I'm not permitted to say, but I will tell you what we do."

"Good. I'm listening."

He clasps his hands together, stretches them out and cracks his knuckles. "We are small group of vigilantes. We work as team to make sure that wrongs are righted. That people who do bad things get what is coming to them."

"So, you're like a gang?"

He winces. "You Americans ... No, we are not a gang. We are an organization with common goal. Professional organization of men. Our goal is to ensure safety of those important to us and to make sure justice is served."

So, they're like a gang. Whether he wants to admit it, Victor is part of a group that engages in criminal activity to further their cause. Wanting your gang to sound more "professional" doesn't change the facts.

"Ok, so you take the law into your own hands. And I get that you can't tell me why I'm here. But he doesn't talk to me. And I want to know why. Is something wrong with his voice?"

Victor shakes his head. "His voice works. He is private man. And he will talk to you when he is ready."

I let my head fall against the wall. It's like talking to a philosopher; every time I ask a question I get an answer that confuses me even more. But there's one thing that sticks in my head and that's the hierarchy. The fact that I'm led by a leash but the other two girls aren't.

"Why does he treat me like a dog? Were the others treated like that before?"

"No, they weren't. You mustn't concern yourself with any other females you see. They have nothing to do with you."

"What does that mean, Victor? Throw me a bone here. Give me a clue." I hug my knees and look up at him, pleading with my eyes. and he does something that surprises me.

He lowers himself to the bed and sits on the floor next to me, kicking his legs out in front of him and crossing his arms.

"The other girls are here because they choose to be. I cannot say any more than that."

"How many others are there?"

"Three. Now two."

So, he collects women, either with bait or a trap. Some of us he leaves caged and others he allows to roam freely. Yeah, makes perfect sense.

"And he leaves me in a room alone to sleep on a dog bed while he lets those others *share* his bed?"

Victor clasps his hands in his lap, quiet. I think that I'm about to get a circular answer.

"Boss had dog once. He found her in dumpster, heard her whimpers as a little puppy. She was the only one of her litter that survived being tossed out like trash."

Bile rises in my throat as I picture innocent creatures being tossed in the garbage. There's a special place in hell for people who do that.

"She followed him everywhere, never left his side. Slept at foot of his bed. Sat on floor as he ate. He took her hunting with him, but not the kind of hunting you are familiar with," he says, flitting his fingers to the side. "He was hunting for enemy. And she warn boss of an impending attack. She … saved his life."

I turn to look at Victor, and his eyes are glassy. I'd swear he was talking about a dog that belonged to him, not his boss.

"She was very special to him. Loyal for twelve years. And then she get cancer. Boss spends almost five thousand dollars in surgery, plus chemotherapy. She died three months later. Then, boss did not leave his room for two weeks." He turns to look at me and my gut twists. "He took better care of Molly than his servants. So being treated like dog is highest praise from boss."

When Victor leaves me alone, I feel different about this, about him. Some of the mystery is gone now and my caped savior is suddenly more human. A man with feelings that go much deeper than anger and impatience.

But he's still a man who is attempting to turn a woman, his captive, into something he can own, someone who will maybe exhibit the same loyalty his canine companion did.

I sleep better my second night here. And when I wake up, I don't see a pair of feet standing near my bed. I feel heavy, though, like it's too early to get up or I slept too hard. But I can't get back to sleep so I run a bath, sinking neck deep in a pile of bubbles.

I keep replaying the scene in my mind of him gripping the girl's throat. And while I felt sorry for her, I can't deny that his power turns me on. His strength and darkness. The control and the way he demands attention and obedience, without saying a fucking word.

And the way he made sure I knew my attacker was dead.

I want to see what's under that cape. I want to see what that kind of power and control looks like.

I get out of the tub and drain the water, wrap the cotton towel around my body. I pull my wet hair into a ponytail.

I hear the click of the door, sounds of men's voices carrying down the hallway, voices I'm not familiar with. I narrow my brow and peek out into my room.

Victor rushes in holding my clothes, my boots dangling from his fingers and his face a pale representation of the man I've come to know over the past few days.

"Get dressed, *fetita*. We must leave, immediately."

"What? Why?" I look behind him, expecting to see someone, maybe secretly hoping it will be him.

"They have found you. And they are coming."

Four months ago~Leigh

You want to fuck with my head? Are you serious?"

I had never pegged Jack for being one to play games. But this was just getting more and more complicated by the minute. I had to hand it to him, though. He was the first guy to actually ask permission to play head games.

"It's not like you think," he said, waving his hands defensively. "Just hear me out."

"I'm right here. Still listening."

"Okay, you've heard about how some women have a rape fantasy, right?"

"Yes."

"Well, I was thinking along those lines, but I've learned that many of those fantasies often bleed over into scenes of violence, and I'm not sure that's something you're up for. But, I think there's something that's deeply connected to the rape fantasy that might really get your engine purring."

I raised my brow. I had never fantasized about being raped, but there were thoughts I'd often had that danced along the fringes of that fantasy. Like maybe having sex with a stranger.

"Like?"

"Like being kidnapped." He said it with the casualness of announcing what was for dinner. "But you won't know when it will happen or where. Maybe I'll be waiting for you one day when you get home from work. I'll tie you up and take you to a hotel, blindfold you and fuck you silly. You'll have no idea who it is, if it's me or one of my friends."

"Wow," I muttered.

"Or maybe I'll get you while you're out having drinks with Andrea. I'll hide in your car, make you take me back to your place. You'll know it's me, of course. You just won't know when I'll show up."

"Go back to the first scenario," I tell him, liking the thought of being blindfolded and not knowing who's pounding into me.

He smiles at me. "Does that mean you're on board?"

"It means I want to think about it. I'm not too crazy about the thought of not knowing when it's coming. I might want to at least have us agree on the day. And if you involve one of your friends, I wouldn't want to know ahead of time. We'd also have to have a safe word. I mean, there are a lot of details to work out, Jack."

"But I'm hearing you right? You want to do this?"

Do I? I'm not sure. But there's no doubt that he's piqued my interest once again. I don't know if this will revive our relationship, but it may be a decent place to start.

"I want to think about doing this, Jack. Let me think about it."

Smiling, Jack cupped my face and kissed my neck. "I'm fucking crazy about you, you know that?"

Eight

I get dressed in my old clothes as fast as I can while Victor provides me instructions. As if they even matter at this point.

"Do as your master tells you, no questions, no matter how crazy it seems. He will take you to safe place."

One of his girls, or his servants, or whatever the fuck she is, brings me my jacket and I slip it on, my heart slamming double time in my chest.

"And one other thing, *fetita*." He cups my face and forces me to look at him. "If anything happens, you run for your life. Silently, and without stopping until you are in public place. Do you understand?"

I nod, feeling my blood run cold.

"Good. Let's go."

I touch the collar around my throat as Victor leads me to the back part of the house and out the door, into the darkness. Jesus, the sun hasn't even come up yet.

Three cars are parked in a line, all running with their headlights glaring ahead. Victor leads me to the one in the middle, opens the back door for me.

"You will be fine, Leigh. *Mult noroc.*"

I slide into the seat, and the car immediately begins to roll forward. To my left, Savior comes into view. He turns to look at me and I glare at him. I don't know why I'm so pissed at him. I think I'm more pissed at all the questions I have.

My mom disappeared for six months when I was twelve, and that's when I decided it was time to lose my virginity. I had too many questions then, too. And since I didn't have the answers I needed, I acted out. Well, right now, I was ready to do something equivalent to losing my virginity in order to understand why my life was in jeopardy.

Savior snaps his fingers at me as we bump down the gravel road, then pops the side of his thigh with his palm. When I don't respond, he pulls me down. My head hits the top of his thigh, and he keeps me pinned in place.

"You want me to go the alternate way, boss?"

"Yes," he replies.

His voice is as deep and commanding as I imagined it to be. My body shudders as it echoes in my head. His thumb whispers across my shoulder. I don't know if he's trying to comfort me with his touch, but it's not working. I'm still pissed as ever.

We round a corner and the driver picks up speed. I turn my gaze to look out the passenger side window. Lights blink and flash. And when we hit a dip in the road, the car bounces violently. I try to sit up, but he pushes me back down. Frustrated, I push up on one arm to reposition myself.

"My shoulder hurts."

He leans down to the floor and passes me a blanket, and I use it to bunch up underneath my neck. I don't know why he won't let me sit up, and I'm tired of not understanding. I keep a look outside through the window, watching tall pine trees whip by as a sliver of orange blinks repeatedly in the distance.

"Will you *please* tell me what's happening?"

I barely catch him looking down at me out of the corner of my eye. He tucks some hair behind my ears, and I slowly turn my head in his direction.

"You're supposed to be addressing me as Master," he growls.

I start to roll my eyes as several pops sound in the distance, immediately followed by the crunch of glass. I instinctively curl into the fetal position when the sounds repeat.

Shit. Someone's shooting at us.

The driver swears and jerks the car hard to the left, punching the gas. The sudden lurch forces me hard against Savior. But when the gun goes off in rapid fire succession, I crawl to the floor. Savior sits still in the seat, his hand pressed against the side of his neck.

"What the fuck!" I cry. "Get down!"

The car abruptly slows as I reach up and grip his cape, pulling him to me. Warm fluid squishes in my hand, sticky as it spreads across my fingers.

Above me, three bullet holes have formed a triangle in the window, right next to where he was sitting.

I scream and the car crashes to a stop, throwing me against the driver's seat. A roaring sound rushes through my ears as I stare at him lying still on the seat.

"Run," he grunts. "Now."

"No," I say. "You're okay. We just…" I twist my head to look at the driver, but I can't see him. I can see several bullet holes in the windshield, though. "Shit."

I hear men yelling outside, their feet crunching in the gravel. The back door jerks open, and I expect to see a double barrel between the eyes. Instead, I see Victor. He sees me on the floor, looks at *him*.

"Boss?"

"I've been hit," he says. "Take her."

"*Fetita*, come with me. Now. There's no time."

Victor grabs me by the wrists and pulls me from the car, the front of which has intersected a tree.

A man slides into the driver's seat as Victor barks orders in Romanian then pulls me across the road in the dark. I hear more gunshots in the distance, and my heart skips double time. We make it to another car and I turn to look at the dark suburban that holds Savior. It backs up, seemingly unaffected by the crash, and gravel flies out from behind the tires as it tears off.

"Get in!" Victor snaps as he runs to the driver's side.

I feel frozen, my blood running cold as I fall into the passenger seat up front.

Now I know why we were all in separate cars: in the hopes that our enemies wouldn't know which one to target. But apparently they found out anyway.

"These people are after me or him?" I ask as Victor guns it.

Small rocks clip the back of the car as we fishtail forward.

"They are after you."

My head hits the headrest as tears scorch the backs of my eyes. I press my index fingers over them, as if that will keep the tears from falling. Then I pull them down, looking at the blood that's starting to dry there.

"Is he going to die?" my voice wavers, and I don't know why I'm so upset about this. I don't know him. I don't know what he looks like or who he is.

But I do know that he saved me in the woods several nights ago. And I know that he sought revenge for my attack and allowed me to watch as he ended the fucker's life.

"I don't know. But one thing is certain, Boris will take good care of him. We have good connections, the best doctors. Don't worry."

I hug myself and close my eyes, praying that I never hear the sound of a gun again.

We make it to the highway as the sun comes up. I don't recognize the area, but I see signs for Liberty, a small town about an hour from my home. I yawn and stretch in the seat as Victor glances my way.

"You want coffee?"

"I *need* coffee," I tell him, feeling my head start to pound from all that's happened.

He nods and points to a sign covered in fast food restaurant logos. "I will stop next exit."

I twist in the seat and turn my thoughts to Savior.

"What is his name, Victor. Who is doing this, and why? Why can't you tell me anything about what's going on?"

I roll my head to the side and look at him. He purses his lips and grips the steering wheel tightly. "I probably could tell you, but boss wishes to do this himself. I can't risk my job. My loyalty to him overshadows your curiosity."

I admire that loyalty. I do. And I share the same loyalty with those who demonstrate their worthiness. Keeping me safe is one thing. But keeping me from the truth is another.

"And if he dies?" I ask, my stomach rolling at the thought. "Will you tell me then?"

Victor jerks back, visibly shocked at my question. "If he dies, then I will tell you everything, yes."

I can tell the thought of that happening physically pains him. "How do you know him anyway?"

"I used to work for his father. I am ... old family friend. I have known him since he was little boy."

His phone buzzes and I glance at the screen. *Boris.* I lift the phone off the console and pass it to him.

"How is he?" Victor asks.

I tense all over as he holds the phone to his ear.

"Mm-hmm ... yes ..."

"Is he okay?" I whisper.

He looks at me, gives a quick nod.

"Good," he says. "Let me know when he's been cleared."

He ends the call and tosses the phone aside.

"He was shot in neck. He seems okay, but the doctors are still examining him."

"Can I see him?"

"No," Victor chuckles. I think it's the first time I've heard him laugh. "You and I will stay somewhere until he is ready to care for you."

"Why do we have to stay so far away? This is ridiculous." My anger is resurfacing, threatening to take over all rational thought.

He shakes his head. "You don't understand. It isn't safe. Until your master can hold you under his wing, we divide and conquer."

I don't know how much conquering we'll do, but I know arguing is pointless. After stopping at a drive-through for coffee and biscuits, Victor pulls out of the restaurant and drives away from the highway, looking out the window at everything we pass: a small elementary school, several churches, a softball field, and an old drug store that looks like the last remodeling job was circa 1950.

"This looks like quiet town. We will stay here for several days, until boss is well."

"I think quiet is an understatement," I say as we pass an abandoned nursing home. "This place is beyond dead."

"Yes. It is good."

"We'll stick out like a sore thumb."

Ignoring me, Victor pulls into the abandoned nursing home, puts the car in park, and picks up his phone.

"I'm going to stretch my legs." I open the door and step out into the crisp air.

"Don't go anywhere," Victor snaps.

I close the door and walk several feet away to the sign that reads *Sunset Manor*. Underneath, letters that once advertised this as "A Retirement Home For Those Who Refuse To Grow Old" have fallen to the ground. The parking lot is split along the curb, sprigs of grass poking from the cracks.

I walk in a circle, kicking up small pieces of gravel with my boots. I look at Victor, who again has the phone pressed to his ear, and I think about how easy it would be to run right now. Victor is small, and he may be fast, but he looks like he's pushing sixty, so I bet I could outrun him.

But where the hell would I go? Back home where they could be waiting for me? I could take off to the gas station down the road, call Andrea, see if she knows anything. I must have been reported missing by now. I was supposed to be at work yesterday. I could tell her that I'm okay, not to worry.

But am I okay? What if the people shooting at us were actually trying to rescue me? What if Savior is the bad guy and we're just running from the good guys?

I look back at Victor, push my hands deep in my pockets. He's watching me like he knows what I'm thinking. Like it's written all over my face.

I think about it some more, the possibility that people are looking for me. But if they were the good guys coming to rescue me, they wouldn't have shot through the window. They would have aimed for the tires or something. They were shooting to kill. And they didn't care if they took out someone other than me in the process.

Realizing how vulnerable I am standing out in the open like this, I hustle back to the car, feeling the chill of the air blow around my face.

When I sit in the passenger seat, the sound of a man's voice comes through Victor's phone so loudly, I can hear almost every word.

"I wouldn't stay there for love or money, man. That's *Jackson's* hometown. You don't think they're going to scour every inch of that place?"

As soon as I hear that name, I snap my head in Victor's direction.

Victor causally glances my way, and I hold my breath as I struggle to hear what else he says. I don't think he knows I can hear him, but he ends the call regardless.

"I have to go. We'll be there soon."

After putting the car in gear, Victor makes his way back towards the interstate. "Boss is fine, just a nick that needed stitches. I'm taking you to him."

I sit in stunned silence as he merges on the highway. I come close, and I mean really close, to asking him if I heard right. That Jack's hometown is the tiny one-street town we just left, and how the fuck is that even relevant to our situation?

But the way he refuses to answer all my other questions, what the hell makes me think he will answer that one? He won't. He'll just deny it. Say that Jack's name never came up. Maybe I did hear him wrong.

But I have a sick feeling that I heard exactly what I think I heard. And Jack may be behind this, somehow.

Three and a half months ago~Jack

I have a favor to ask, and before you say no, just hear me out. There's money involved."

Arrow leaned against the window frame, his attention diverted outside. He was obviously distracted, and I began to wonder if I should have come today.

"I rarely say no without hearing someone out, Jackson. You know that."

I beg to differ. But no fucking way was I arguing with this dude. I'd known him long enough to know that he wouldn't hesitate to say no before hearing the whole story.

"Sorry. I didn't mean any disrespect. Anyway, this favor is more like a job, in that I'm willing to pay." I stood up and walked behind the chair. I gripped the back, feeling suddenly nervous. I wanted this. Really fucking wanted this. "My girlfriend and I want to role play this little fantasy she's had. Well, we've both had, if I'm being honest."

Arrow looked at me, his eyes pointed down, narrowing. Shit, I could tell he wasn't in the mood.

I held my hands up. "She wants to be kidnapped. We've discussed a few of the details, and she's down with all kinds of mind fuckery. I wanted to ask you, since you have the perfect setup for it here, if you'd be willing to do the deed, bring her here."

He chuckled and turned around, sat down at his desk, shaking his head. I sat across from him. Now we were eye level.

"What deed would I be doing, exactly?" he asked, leaning back in his chair. "Kidnapping, fucking, or both?"

Fuck, I'd always respected the hell out of Arrow, but hearing him talk about fucking my girl made me want to fight. I bit the edges of my lips and gripped the armrests.

"Not really down with anyone else fucking her, but thanks for asking. I was thinking you could get her, put her in the dungeon room. I'd want her to be held for about a day, so someone would need to look out for her, feed her, that kind of shit."

Arrow wiped the corners of his mouth, studied me hard for a moment like he was considering it. "I'm remodeling my dungeon. Turning it into the master suite."

"I'm willing to pay two grand. And it really doesn't matter where you keep her. Shit, toss her in the attic," I said, laughing. Seriously, it really did not matter. My dick hardened as I thought about Leigh being scared but also getting wet, just knowing I'm coming for her.

I could let Arrow fuck her, if I so fucking chose. She would know it wasn't me, though. All men fuck differently. Then again, I could fuck her different from my normal style, make her *think* it was someone else. Now there was an idea.

"Two grand isn't much for that kind of job. What if she turns on you, decides after the fact that she really didn't want it after all? Have you thought this through?"

I raked my hands through my hair, pushed out a hard breath. "Yes, I've thought it through. Leigh isn't the kind of chick that would turn on anyone, much less her boyfriend. Trust me. She's into this shit. Craves it."

Arrow looked at me, stroking his chin, doubt dancing in his eyes. Obviously, he needed a push. Let's see if I have what it takes to give him that push he needs. "So, what kind of money are we talking here?"

He picked up a pen, tapped the tip of it rhythmically against a small sticky note on his desk. "Come back to me with something in the five figures, and we'll continue this conversation."

Stunned, I didn't know whether to laugh or ask him if he'd lost his fucking crackers. He had to be joking. But nope. Not joking. There was no way I could afford something like that. It would clean out all my savings. Hell, I was hesitant to offer two thousand, but I figured he wouldn't do it for less than that.

I started to tell him to go to hell. Fuck, I could have hired a god damn hooker to roleplay a kidnap fantasy for probably a couple hundred. My pulse hammered as my anger rose. But then I came up with a spur of the moment plan.

"You know I don't have that kind of dough, man. There's got to be something we can work out. Some kind of trade, maybe?"

He raised a brow, dropped the pen. "What can you do for me that one of my men can't?"

I shrugged. "You tell me."

Arrow studied me for a minute, and I sifted through thoughts, ideas. What *could* I do that his men couldn't?

I had known Arrow for almost ten years. My older brother used to work for him when Arrow ran a private investigation firm. But Arrow's dad, a real estate mogul, had died, leaving Arrow millions. He still owns the firm, but it's mostly hands off at this point. And given what he did in his spare time, and the fact that he employed half a dozen men or so to assist him and take care of his dirty work, there probably wasn't a very good chance that I had anything worth trading. Except my skills as a construction worker.

"You mentioned converting your dungeon into a master bedroom. I can help out with that. You know I can build a house from the ground up."

He flashed a half smile. "Yeah, I know you're good with your hands, Jackson. But I got a contractor taking care of it already. I think there's something else you may be able to do for me."

"Shit, okay. Name it."

"I was going to bring this up with one of my guys tomorrow. But I actually think you'd be a good candidate. Better, in fact."

"Sounds promising."

He sat forward in his chair, weaving the pen through alternating fingers.

"Torrin has a new girlfriend. Just found out last week."

"Torrin Grainger? You still keeping track of that fucker?" I knew there was bad blood between them. Torrin had knocked up Arrow's baby sister not long ago. I don't know all the details, but apparently she and the baby died during childbirth, and Arrow held him personally responsible.

"Yeah. I've been waiting for the perfect opportunity to drop a bomb. And I think that opportunity just knocked on my fucking door."

"Great," I said. "What can I do?"

He narrowed his eyes at me, glanced down at my hands as if wondering if I was strong enough for the job.

"You can bring me his girlfriend."

I waited for more, sure that wasn't all he wanted.

"And?" I asked.

"And, that's it. She works at that diner on King Street. The afternoon shift. I want you to hang out, flirt with her. Ask her out for a beer. If she seems resistant, which I doubt she will with your good looks, just tell her a friend of yours has some chocolate rock. I swear to fucking god, she'll follow you to your car panting. Bring her here, and I'll handle the rest."

My gut sank in nervousness. Arrow was not the kind to drop gentle bombs. I couldn't help but wonder what he had planned for her.

"Seems simple enough, I guess. Is that all? You just want me to bring her here? Nothing else?"

He nodded.

"What, uh, what are you going to do to her?" I almost cringed asking the question.

Arrow gave me a dismissive wave. "I just want to talk with her. Maybe give that fucking boyfriend of hers a scare. Don't worry about that. Once you get her to me, your job will be done, and I'll take care of your request."

This was almost too good to be true. It seemed to me that two grand should have been worth more to him than a simple conversation with Torrin's bitch of the month. But flirting with some random broad and taking her for a ride to his house was totally doable. And easy.

"Okay. I'll do it. When is she working next?"

Nine

I think about the way my father took care of me when I was little, before he died of lung cancer. And I think about Savior slicing my attacker's throat. My father was a gentle, loving man, but I have no doubt that he would have gone to extremes like that to protect me if someone had assaulted me.

"Are you nervous, *fetita*?"

I stop bouncing my leg, suddenly aware of the energy I'm giving off. "No. Just restless. I think I had too much coffee." Too much coffee following a string of bullets flying my way. I glance at my hand, at the small amount of blood still stuck underneath my fingernails. I had washed them at a gas station bathroom, but the remnants remained.

"We'll be there in ten minutes. Then you can stretch your legs."

I let my head fall against the back of the seat and stretch my arms out in front of me.

"You never told me where he is. We're not going back to his house, right?"

"No, not yet. The area must be secured, as well as the people responsible."

"How do you secure people?" I ask him.

He gives me a wary look.

"Oh. Never mind."

Victor takes the first exit off the highway, and we finally get to a home that's secluded behind a thick barrier of woods. As soon as we walk inside the house, I can feel his presence.

"Is anyone else here?" I ask Victor.

"Boris."

"What about..." I tense up, thinking about the woman he pressed against the wall yesterday.

"I'm not sure."

Victor opens a door that leads to a basement, and Boris passes us on the way down.

At the foot of the stairs is a small table holding a lamp that barely illuminates the space around us. At the other end of the room, he melts into the darkness, deep in a sofa chair and wearing that god damn cape. That thing was sexy for five minutes, but I'm so fucking sick of it, ready to see what's underneath. Next to the chair, on the floor, is a fluffy pet bed, resembling the one I had at his house. But this one is turquoise.

Victor walks to him and he stands. I stay near the foot of the stairs, close to the light.

"You look better than the last time I saw you."

"I feel better."

Victor looks at me, then back to Savior. "If you were to ask my opinion, I would say that she is ready, boss."

Turning his head slightly to the side, he looks my way. Even though I can't see his eyes on me, I can feel them.

"Are we still on for the preparations?"

"Yes, Victor. Nothing has changed."

"Good. I'm ready to ... what is that expression you use? Wrap this up?"

Savior reaches out to shake his hand and Victor chuckles softly. "Call if you need anything. I'll be back before this evening."

When he walks past me, Victor pauses, cups his hand to my cheek. Lifts his lips in a smile. He then disappears upstairs, leaving me alone with him once again.

I glance up at him, take a few tentative steps. He does the same, though his steps are much less tentative than mine.

He holds out his hand. "Come, sit with me."

"No," I say. My heart bangs inside my chest. And I'm surprised at my own defiance. But it's officially there.

His body stiffens and his hand drops. I'm sure he's about to hit something again. But for whatever reason, I don't care.

He walks to the side of the chair and pushes the bed around until it's directly at his feet. "Sit," he snaps, pointing at the fluffy material.

I stand my ground. "I'm not a pet you can bark orders at."

His arms cross behind his back, and I watch his chest slowly expand as he takes in a deep breath, keeping his face pointed at me, the same way it was when he slit my attacker's throat. I feel hot all over, an ache starting to consume me.

"I am not going to say it again," he grumbles, teeth clenched.

I glance down, see his right hand as it balls up into a fist, then releases, over and over.

"And you can't seriously expect me to comply, to keep kneeling at your feet without an explanation as to why I'm here. That kind of respect is earned."

He ticks his head to the side, steps closer to me. I feel my stomach knot up, bracing myself for the worst. "You don't know what you're asking," he says.

"Then enlighten me."

It's then that my eyes finally adjust to the lighting. I can see one of his eyes through the mesh, dark and angry as it searches my face.

It's barely perceptible, but I hear him growl. And then he barges past me, brushing against my arm. I turn his way, astonished that he's actually walking away from me.

"If someone were trying to kill you, wouldn't you want to know who they were, and why?" He freezes, turns his head in my direction. "Well, I want to know, and I want to see your face when you tell me. Until then, I will not sit, or stay, or call you Master."

He stands still for a moment, then walks up the stairs, two at a time. I know he's angry. I can feel it in the wake of his departure. And while a part of me fears his return, the other part is pretty confident he won't do anything to hurt me.

The women who were at his house were there willingly. All of them except me. I was chosen for some reason. And I want to know what that reason is. Until then, I wait him out.

———

I end up drifting off in the leather chair with my legs curled up underneath me. It feels good to have something other than a dog bed underneath my ass for a change. But when I wake up, my neck is stiff and my body aches.

I hear noises coming from upstairs, and moments later, the basement door opens. His cape drifts behind him as he floats down the steps.

I swivel my legs around and down to the floor before standing up a little too quickly. I feel woozy for a second but gain my footing the moment I see him unwrap the dark material from his body. He tosses the black fabric to the floor like it means nothing.

He's just as big without the cape as he is with it. In fact, maybe bigger. I find myself swallowing hard as I take in the sculpted muscles of his arms and the way his green cotton shirt stretches against his abs and biceps.

How? is the first question that comes to mind. *How can you hide that amazing body?*

"Uh," I mutter, visually licking him from head to toe.

And then he reaches up with one hand, grips the top of the hood, and gently pulls it from his head.

My chest is an orchestra of drum beats as I stare like a dumbstruck teen.

He pulls the hood off completely and lets it fall to the floor.

I pull in a gasp, take a step back, then immediately regret my reaction. I gulp and pull my lips inside my mouth to fight my own horror at what I see. Well, at least now I know why he kept himself hidden.

One half of his face is … perfect. Beautiful. Stubble decorates a strong chin, and my gaze trails up to hazel eyes staring back at me with honest trepidation.

It's *that* half I wish I could focus on.

The other half of his face is a series of mangled scars, twisting in on themselves like broken branches of a tree. It's utterly hideous.

It's *this* half I want to touch.

I follow the scars in a loop with my eyes, licking my lips. Then I feel bad for staring, so I make eye contact again.

He walks to me, stops a foot away, lifts my right hand and presses it to his cheek. I start to pull away, but he doesn't let me. Brings it right back.

"Does it hurt?" I ask, angling my head up at him.

He shakes a *no*.

The scars don't look fresh, but they don't look very old either. I can still see the dots where the stitches were. I let my fingers run over the surface of his bumpy flesh, trailing every line as if it has a story to tell that can only be read with a touch. The bandage still rests on his neck, a small red dot in the center of the pad.

"How did this happen?"

"Enemies and carelessness. I was pinned to a wall. And when I turned my head, they came at me with a homemade whip with blades on the end."

I cringe at the thought, drop my hand, touch my fingertips together. "The same ones that are after me?"

"Yes. The same ones that are after you."

"But why? Why would your enemies be after me? There's no connection between us whatsoever. Is there?"

He spins, runs his hands through his hair, paces. I watch him move, feeling the heat build between my legs.

"Torrin Grainger and I have been enemies for years. There's bad blood there, and ultimately, he wants me, not you. But he knows one way to get to me is by killing you."

My body turns to ice. "Why? Why would killing me get to you? You don't even know me. Or you didn't."

"I know enough," he snaps.

"Like?"

He bulldozes his way back to me, grips the back of my head with tight fists, tugging my hair. "Like you belong to me," he growls.

I press my palms against his chest as his eyes search my face. He leans close, presses his lips against mine. I coil back, the intensity overwhelming. As his tongue pushes inside my mouth, I know I'll give in if I let this continue. My body aches as my hands spread down. I feel the ridges of his muscles against my fingertips and I want him more than ever.

Which is exactly why I have to stop him.

I give a hard thrust and he doesn't budge an inch. But our lips become unstuck.

"No," I say. "You can't just say I belong to you and expect me to melt into a puddle. It doesn't work like that."

Not anymore, anyway. I've let my hormones dictate way too much in my life. And right now, they're threatening to take over once again, just like they did with Jack.

"Watch me," he grumbles, running his hands down my back and cupping my ass.

I pull in a sharp breath and he presses his body against mine. His erection is hard on my belly, and it makes the ache between my legs pulsate.

"Tell me you don't want me right now," he bellows.

His breath is warm on my face. I glance at his scars, wondering if they're concealing something that lies underneath or showing the real man.

I fight the demon inside of me, the demon that wants to let him take me. The demon that imagines him slamming me to the floor and fucking me until I'm weary. But all these things I have imagined before. And they did nothing but fuck me over. I don't want to feel those things anymore.

"I don't want you right now," I answer.

His eyes flair, and he backs away, flinging his arms to his side. "Liar."

I scan his face, not wanting to miss the hurt there, if it's there. But all I see is anger.

"I still don't know enough. And I will not make the same mistake I've made countless times. You want me? You earn it."

I walk past him, eyes growing at my own ability to be so outspoken. But he grabs my shirt and pulls me back.

"Hey," he barks.

I spin on my heels, throw his hands aside.

"I saved you," he grumbles.

"I didn't ask you to."

A smirk tugs at his lips. He tosses his head back and belts out a laugh.

I narrow my eyes.

Mother fucker.

"Would you like for one of my men to take you back to your special hiking place?"

"Fine with me," I say. "In fact, you can even wait until it gets dark. My family is probably wondering where the hell I am."

His smile fades. He cocks his head. "What family, Leigh? Your parents are gone, you have no brothers or sisters, and your mom's family has nothing to do with her or you. You don't have a boyfriend, and your friend, Andrea, as well as all your co-workers, think that you're visiting a dying relative in San Antonio."

He lifts a cell phone from his pocket, and I immediately recognize it as mine. I try to swipe it from his grasp, but he jerks it away too fast.

"Why would she think that?" I snap.

"Because. That's what I told her. Sent her a message from one of your little apps. Imagine how delighted I was to find this lying on the trail."

Bubbles of rage simmer deep in my gut, and my head pounds as my anger builds. I grit my teeth, glare at him with all the hatred in the world.

"Fuck you." My voice is an angry growl.

He lifts one brow at me, sliding the phone back in his pocket. "Fuck *me*?" he asks.

"Yes," I spit. "Fuck. You."

His lips curl again. "Fine. Have it your way."

He bends at the waist and grabs my thighs, lifts me off the floor and tosses me over his shoulder. Without so much as a strained breath, he carries me upstairs and down a long hallway and into a bedroom. My body is tossed on top of a bed, and by the time I look up, he's walking out of the room, slamming the door. I scoot against the headboard and wonder if this is some sort of solitary confinement type of punishment.

But he comes back to the room moments later with a belt, and I know what that's for.

He flips me onto my front and tugs the waist of my jeans down. I don't try to stop him and it's not because I know I'll lose. It's because I don't want to stop him.

I reach above my head, grip the comforter. Wait for the first blow.

The leather strikes my flesh with a searing pain that makes my mouth fall open. I squeeze my eyes shut, determined not to make a sound.

The second hit makes me huff. The strike reverberates off the walls, makes my ears hum.

The third slap makes my body jerk. I let out a yelp.

"That's more like it," he grunts.

He wants to hear that he's hurting me. I bite my lower lip, not quite ready to give him the satisfaction. But when the belt sears into my flesh the fourth time, and I taste my own blood from biting my lip too hard, tears burn my eyes and I let out a painful groan.

I feel him drag the edge of the leather across my skin, forcing my body to tingle. He lies the belt across my backside and I feel the mattress give underneath me as the belt presses into my tender flesh. His face lowers to my neck and he bites me so hard my nipples pucker into tight points. And then his weight lifts and I catch my breath, heart beating wild in my chest.

I focus on the sounds of his breathing, trying to make my own slow down as I feel the flames dance on my ass. But the silence is gone as the belt explodes against me a final time, the pain so enormous I cry out uncontrollably.

My body coils up tight as he walks around to the other side of the bed and slides his fingers under my hand, releasing the death grip I have on the comforter. He pulls my pants back up, and when he rolls me over, I look up at him, staring down at me holding the belt. He lifts my arm off the bed and tugs me to the headboard. But not before encircling my wrists with the brown leather that was just subduing me in a way that no man ever had without laying hands on me.

I snap my head in time to see that he's securing the metal loop of the belt to an O-ring mounted on the wall. My gaze wanders down his body as he stands next to me. I wait breathlessly for his next move. When he's done, he walks to the foot of the bed, grips the button of his jeans and snaps them loose.

"Fuck *me*, huh?"

I bend my wrist and grip the belt, using it as leverage as I pull myself up higher on the bed. And I silently curse myself for being so turned on. But I can't stop watching him with a hunger that I know has to be written all over my face as he drops his pants to the floor. I force my gaze up, refusing to give in. Yes, I want it. No, I don't need it.

"Still don't want me?" he asks, crossing his arms and tugging his shirt over his head.

His chest and abs punch me with their perfection and I can't help but laugh. The man must spend two hours a day working out to maintain a body like that. And I don't know why I'm laughing right now because there is nothing about this that is even remotely funny. Want turns to need and ripples through every bone in my body as I drink him in.

He takes a step, bumps into the foot of the bed. "Answer my question, Leigh. You still don't want me?" He leans forward, pushes his fists into the mattress.

Fuck, I want him with all that is in me. But I want to see just how far I can push him. And how much he will push back. I bite the inside of my lip as I start to nod. But fortunately, my head moves side to side in a *no* as I glare ahead.

The scarred side of his face twitches. He grips the waist band of his underwear and peels them down. After picking up his clothes from the floor, he faces me again. I've never found dicks to be particularly attractive. At least not the way other body parts are, like abs and pecs, asses, and even tits. Let's be honest here; you don't have to be attracted to women to appreciate the swell of a bosom, the delicateness of a nipple, or the slope of her chest.

But damn it all to hell, the way his erection bounces as he walks my way has me licking my lips. He's big, thick, and the head is perfectly proportioned to the size of his shaft. It looks like it could do some damage. And it kind of already is since it's making me want to say fuck it, I'll just forget everything I promised myself. And forget that he's stolen my phone, posed as me, and lied to my best friend.

Once I let him know he has me, it's all over. I'll lose myself yet again in a vortex of bullshit and making compromises I shouldn't make.

And I don't even know this man's name.

"No. I still don't want you."

He straightens his back, fists at his side. He knows I'm lying. This is just a game. Let's see what his next move is.

After walking to the door, he twists the knob and steps out, pulling the door closed. But he returns seconds later with a woman, unclothed just like he is. I don't recognize her from last night. Her hair is dark auburn, and she's just a sliver of a girl, with the exception of being well-endowed above the waist.

He spins her around so that her back is to me and grips the back of her head with one hand. His other moves down her spine as he kisses her. I can see her body respond to him. She relaxes, lets her arms move down his sides, stopping at his pelvis. Her groans are audible as he squeezes her ass cheek and fists her hair tightly.

"Her insubordination is your reward," he tells her, nodding in my direction.

She giggles, looks down towards his erection. "Master, you look like you're ready for action."

He pulls her to his chest, presses her head to his pecs, and bores his gaze into me. "I am. And today, let's show our friend what action looks like."

Waves of heat ripple between my legs as he picks her up off the floor and carries her to the wall next to the bed. He then lifts her higher, tossing her legs over his shoulder. She cries out and grips the top of his head as she falls against the wall behind her. His face moves between her legs, the sounds of his sucking only partially overshadowed by her moans of pleasure.

Jesus. I watch him push his fingers deep inside of her. His arm pumps furiously, loud squelching sounds leaving no doubt as to what he's doing. The woman's face morphs into one of pleasure. Back and forth movements of his head bring her close.

"May I come, Master?" she huffs.

He pauses, looks at her, slows his arm.

Then he looks at me. "Today, you can come whenever you like, as much as you like."

I hold his stare, feeling my face warm, heat traveling down the front of me. But then he pulls his gaze away and returns to his feast.

I watch the way her body responds. She doesn't look at me once. Her eyes close, and her nipples draw up tight as she begins to rock her hips against his face. Holding tight to his hair, she starts to shake, and her thighs quiver. He fucks her harder with his hand, and her orgasm seems to slam into her at once. She screams and her head hits the wall.

He relents some, backing away from her but keeping his hands on her bottom. Then he slides her down slowly, moving his fists to her breasts and cupping them. He leans down to lick them, and the woman smiles, laughs.

"Thank you, Master," she whispers.

I don't know what the point of his little show is. To taunt me? Make me want him more? Punish me? I'm not sure how I feel about this.

But he seems to be trying to up the ante when he brings her to the bed and forces her face down, ass up.

I draw my feet up, giving her room. He's facing me when he enters her from behind. I watch him place his hands on her ass, glide them to her hips, grip tightly. Arousal blooms between my legs.

Her hands slowly grasp the soft comforter. He leans forward and pulls her arms to her backside, holding her wrists to her lower back.

He enters her, eyes on me as his body begins to rock. I stare back for several seconds, but the tension between us is damn near palpable. I shake my head and look away. The woman huffs, moans, cries, groans. But he doesn't make a sound. Not one indication that he's enjoying this.

His hands tighten around her wrists, and he repositions them before slamming into her with force. Her hair moves along the comforter, and the sounds of their flesh slapping together become a symphony.

When his head rolls back, I know he's close. The look on his face is unmistakable. The unscarred side twists, tightens. And then he pulls out of her and rubs the lower part of his cock along the swell of her ass, hard jets of fluid spurting on her flesh in ribbons of white.

It's the sight of him coming on her ass that turns me on the most, and the way the thick ropes of fluid pool in the divots of her body. He takes his palm and smears it all along her skin. She laughs softly.

"Was that three orgasms I counted?" he asks her.

"Yes," she answers. "Thank you, Master."

After he finishes rubbing his seed into her flesh, he flicks his gaze at me again. I grip the belt above me and raise my brows at him.

Yeah? Now what?

"Go take a bath," he says to her. "I'll be in there shortly."

She pushes herself up and, avoiding my stare, walks out of the room.

I have so many things to say, I don't know where to start.

"That was ... fascinating. I'm surprised you didn't charge me admission."

He picks up his shirt off the floor, wipes his crotch. "You're an ungrateful shit."

"Ungrateful? That you're holding me against my will and subjecting me to watching you fuck one of your little playthings?"

"To keep you safe!" he yells, leaning down and narrowing his eyes at me.

I pull in a deep breath. "Yeah, you keep saying that, but I still don't know how I've gotten tangled up in the webs *you've* weaved." I pull myself up higher, my heart drumming like mad. "And furthermore, you've had my phone this whole time. You could have at least told me you found it." His forehead vein bumps as I continue, his face turning dark red. "And if you think that I will continue to prance around half naked wearing some stupid fucking collar just because you lost your dog, you better think again."

His face relaxes, and his jaw clicks. Hurt swims in his eyes as they start to sag. He stands up, drops his gaze to the bed, licks his lips. My stomach clenches tight as I realize I've just struck a very tender nerve. Maybe I went overboard.

"I ... I didn't mean it like that." I think of something to say to cover up my giant assholery. But he doesn't give me enough time. He swipes his clothes off the floor and disappears out of the room.

I should feel proud that I've learned what his below-the-belt is. But I don't. I feel guilty as hell. I feel sick that I've allowed myself to lash out so verbally. It isn't like me. But I'm not sure what he expects from someone who's being held hostage.

Seconds later, he barges back in and undoes the belt, tossing it aside before leaving me alone again.

I'm not sure what I'm supposed to do, where I should go. Like my whole fucking life now, everything is one giant question. So I stay in the room the rest of the day.

Victor knocks on my door sometime during the afternoon, asking me if I want lunch, but I tell him no. I'm not hungry. I'm angry and confused. And I just want to go back home, back to my normal life.

I fall asleep again, and when I wake up, the room is blanketed in the shadows of a setting sun. I spread the blinds apart and look outside. The skies above look gray and forlorn.

Victor pokes his head in the room. "Time to eat, *fetita*."

Grumbling and sore, I roll out from underneath the covers. My mouth is tacky and my head is pounding.

"Are you hungry?" Victor asks.

"I don't know."

He places a sympathetic hand on my back before leading me down the hall and into the kitchen.

Savior is already at the table, along with his little fuck buddy and Boris. I'm just the odd man out. I can feel the tension growing as I sit down in the only vacant seat. Her, *Boobs*, to my right, smiling like it's her fucking wedding reception or some shit, and him, all the way across the table. Stiff and silent.

I glance up and see his eyes, hollow at they stare at the table. Scattered around are half a dozen takeout boxes from a Chinese restaurant. Nobody's reaching for any food.

"Well, we are a lively bunch tonight," Victor says.

I blow out a weary breath.

Boris reaches for the first box. "I'll start. I'm hungry as a polar bear in winter."

Boobs snickers. And I have to admit it did sound funny. But laughing is the last thing I have the urge to do.

"I thought tonight we would be celebrating the fact that boss is all right."

And me. Don't forget about me: the person they were after to begin with.

"I'm relieved that Master is okay, too." Boobs rests her hand next to his on the table. I glare at her, thinking that if I have to hear the word Master one more time I will stab my ears with this fork I'm holding. I feel my nostrils curl, then flick my gaze at him.

He's watching me, and I'm sure he sees my irritation. I put on my poker face, trying to act like I don't care.

"Lo Mein?" Victor asks, holding a white box in my direction.

"Sure," I mumble, dumping some onto my plate.

No one talks while we eat, with the exception of Boobs who just has to point out how delicious everything is. I'm at a loss as to why she's not standing over him, serving him food, pouring his drinks like the other two were last night. In fact, she's not even wearing a collar, now that I've taken the time to look.

Whatever. I don't care. Fucker has my phone, my connection to the outside world. And all the secrets that are keeping me here.

Victor and Boris finish eating first. And when they get up and leave the three of us alone, my stomach twists up into knots. I can't sit here with them.

I drink the rest of my water and stand up. But before I leave, I look at him one more time. He's sliding his fingernail between his teeth, the scars on his face stretched as he curls one side of his lip up. I flash back to this morning, when he was shot and he told me to run. And I just want to cry.

"I shouldn't have said what I did earlier. I'm sorry. About what I said and your dog."

I take my plate and glass and walk into the kitchen without waiting for him to respond, or to not respond. Victor is putting his plate in a dishwasher.

"What happened between you two?" he asks me.

"He didn't tell you?"

Victor wipes his hands on a towel and tosses it over his shoulder. "I have been in and out all day. He has told me nothing. Although I do see he has chosen to reveal his face to you. That is good sign."

I start to unload on Victor, tell him about the phone, that I know his enemies are after me to get to him, and that I made a stupid comment about his dog. But I know it will just get me worked up again.

"It doesn't matter," I say. "Besides, he'll tell you if he wants you to know."

It should feel good to give Victor a taste of his own medicine, but it doesn't. I walk out of the kitchen, bypassing the dining room, and make my way back to the bedroom I was in earlier.

I end up rummaging through the bedside table, looking for something to read. I'd settle for a goddamn diary at this point. I'm so fucking bored, I feel like I'm going to lose what little sanity I have left.

I consider leaving for a second. Just walking out of here and heading for the main road or a neighbor's house. And it seems very enticing. But there's that little voice in my head that tells me that would be a mistake.

I don't find anything in the bedside table, so I head to the closet.

Bingo!

On the floor is a box of magazines. I reach inside and pull it out, excited as fuck to have words in front of me. Smiling, I pull out the one on top, thinking it's a *Cosmo* but finding out pretty quickly it's actually *Hustler*. That's okay. *Hustler* has articles.

I flop back on the bed and start thumbing through the pages when I hear a knock at the door.

"Yeah?"

He appears, walks inside and starts to say something when he freezes. His eyes have dropped to the magazine I'm holding.

"There's a whole boxful if you want one."

He rakes his hand through his hair. "No. Just wasn't expecting to see that."

After pushing his fists in his pockets, he lets his gaze move from the box on the floor to the closet. "This is Boris's room. You're going to have to relocate."

I toss the magazine aside. "Where to?"

"Basement or the floor of my room. Your choice."

"The *floor*?" I ask, dumbfounded. What the fuck?

"I'll bring the bed up if you wish. But yes. You can sleep on the pet bed, or you can have the basement to yourself."

"Pfft. I'm not sleeping in the same room as you and Boobs."

"Boobs?"

"Your girlfriend. I don't know her name any more than I know yours."

"She's not my girlfriend. And she went home."

"What happened? She mouth off, too? Did you push her against the wall and scare the piss out of her?"

He barges over to me, grips the side of my face, and pushes me down on the bed, his body hovering above me. Excitement surges through me as I hold back a smile.

"I'm getting a little tired of that mouth of yours. I've got a good mind to shove something inside of it to shut you up."

My pussy throbs, arousal leaking from me as he huffs an angry breath in my face. I hope he does shove his cock in my mouth, take me, shut me up. Strip me of any choice in the matter. I dart my eyes around his, seeing the fury there in the dark green and brown flecks.

Fuck, he's perfect right now. Perfect when he takes control like *this*.

I feel my face pulse, and he lets up. My chest is heaving, my cunt throbbing.

He gives my cheek a slap, but it isn't that hard. It's just enough to force a moan to escape my throat. A moan he hears.

His eyes flicker, like he recognizes something in that moan. And then he stands up.

"I'm making a decision for you. You'll sleep in the basement." He scoops me off the bed and tosses me over his shoulder, carries me downstairs. I spend the whole time staring at his ass, imagining what it would feel like while he's fucking me. Hardening as he pushes, then softening as he pulls out.

He drops me in the chair and turns to leave.

"What if I get hungry? Or thirsty?"

He flips his head to the side. "Then go upstairs and get something to eat. Contrary to what you think, Leigh, you're really not my prisoner."

———

I settle onto the chair, pulling the blanket up to my neck. It's fucking cold as shit down here, something I neglected to consider before being a bitch once again to the man who had saved me. But my belly is full of cold Chinese food that I just snacked on, and I have a non-serrated steak knife in my pocket, just in case any more drama unfolds during the night. I don't know if I would use it on someone, but it makes me feel safer, and that's all that matters.

I drift to sleep, leaving the small lamp on, touching the collar around my neck a few times before unconsciousness takes me. Weird dreams start up right away. But eventually, I find myself in a tropical location, taking snapshots of a brilliant sunset from a tour bus.

And that's when I wake up to arms lifting me from the chair. I open my eyes, confused but not scared. And when I see that it's him, I know that whatever he's doing, his intentions are in the right place. With the blanket and all, he carries me up the flight of steps. I have my arms wrapped around his neck, on his good side, so I stare at the part of him that hasn't been butchered by enemies he's made for one reason or another.

He takes me into his bedroom, kicking the door shut behind him. A small nightlight casts enough of a glow that I can see the sheets are disheveled. He sets me on the edge of the bed and lifts both arms before pulling off my shirt. Remembering the knife in my back pocket, I'm suddenly terrified of what he will think if he sees it. I yank it out and slide it behind me before he has a chance to spot it.

He leans down and unbuttons my jeans. I'm too fucking tired to stop him. If I even wanted to. Which I don't.

I fall backwards on the bed and let him do the rest, wondering what's different about this time. Why I'm not resisting him like I did earlier when he said I belonged to him. Maybe I am crazy.

I watch his eyes looking at my body as he pulls my pants over my ankles. I'm still in my bra and underwear, and I expect him to make me take those off, but he doesn't. He simply steps out of his long flannel pants and tells me to slide over.

I do, putting my hand over the knife and sliding it under my pillow. I roll onto my side as the bed bounces around. And then his arm comes around me, his leg flops over my hip, and his lips press to my ear.

"I've gone about this the wrong way," he says.

His breath tickles my ear, and waves of desire ripple through me. I start to ask him what he means, but I figure he's headed in that direction. He pulls me so close to him that I can feel his heart beating inside his chest. I try to pry his arm off but he hugs me tighter. I only want to face him.

"Stop fighting me. You wanted to know why you're here. I'm going to tell you everything. And I'm going to keep you close while I do."

"Why?" I ask.

"Because. You're not going to like it."

I turned to look at the chick sitting next to me. She was damn fine, and I decided that she might be willing to put out for a little chocolate rock.

"You know, I'm doing you quite a favor," I told her.

She smiled at me, placed her hand on my leg. "I know that. And I appreciate the hookup. My boyfriend will definitely be interested, too."

I pulled into Arrow's driveway, the trees obscuring his house until we were right up on it. I put the car in park and turned off the engine.

"What say you give me a little thank-you right now?" I asked, twisting in the seat to face her as I gave my jeans button a tug. Erin looked out the windshield, as if she was worried someone would see. "No one will bother us, trust me. Come on, just a quick suck. I'll even convince my buddy you should get extra for the same price. He's cool like that."

Erin licked her lips. Hitting it off with her had been a breeze. She was a real slut, through and through. Hell, we had only talked all of fifteen minutes before she leaned over the edge of the counter to show off her cleavage, spilling out of her diner uniform. When I told her she should come with me after her shift to party, she was all over that shit. And now? She was going to suck me off for a little heroin and crack mixture I wasn't even sure she'd get.

I pulled out my cock and she lowered her head. Damn, she was almost as easy as Leigh had been that first night I met her. Bitches were stupid. Maybe I should get rid of Leigh and trade her in for Erin. She might be down with all the shit that Leigh wasn't down with.

I pushed her head all the way down as I emptied myself. She coughed a few times, but I pushed harder, making sure every last spurt went down her throat. When she resurfaced, I could see the glassiness in her eyes.

"Can we go in now?"

"Yep." I zipped up my pants and led her to the front door.

Arrow answered within seconds. I had told Erin that his face was a little scarred, but she still reacted when she saw him. It was subtle, but she took a step back.

"How's it going?"

Arrow darted his gaze back and forth between the two of us, then opened the door all the way to let us in. We followed him to the living room where he sat down, spreading his arms across the back of his sofa and nodding for us to join him.

Erin and I sat, side by side.

"How's business?" Arrow asked me.

"Good, good. Been busier than usual." I sure hoped he wasn't going to drag this out. All he told me to do was bring her here, and I didn't feel like going through any motions.

"Tell me about your friend here."

I swallowed and looked at Erin. She flashed a nervous smile.

"Oh, this is Erin. She works at Chuchu's Diner in Germanton. We were both, uh, you know, like I said, wanting to party tonight."

"Here?" Arrow asked, his face one of total fucking shock.

"Hell no. Not here. Back at my place. With some of your choco rocko, you know?"

Jesus. Had he forgotten the deal we made?

"Ah," he finally said. "Choco rocko. Good shit. It'll fuck you up, though. You sure?"

I twisted towards him, flickered my eyes like *dude*. "Yeah. We're sure. Right, Erin?" I looked at her and she nodded extremely enthusiastically. "Yep. We're one hundred and ten percent sure."

Arrow smirked. Then he looked at Erin, leaning forward and clasping his hands together. "Erin?"

"Yes?"

"Jack here has had the privilege of sampling the goods. How would you like to do the same before you commit to buying?"

"Are you serious? Like, a *free* sample? Right now?"

Arrow nodded.

"Damn. How can I say no to that?"

Arrow glanced behind us and gestured at someone with the flick of a finger. "Why don't you go with this gentleman, Erin. He'll take good care of you."

I watched her walk down the hallway with some tall dude I didn't recognize. When she was out of sight, I turned to Arrow. "That was way too fucking easy, man. Guess I shouldn't admit it. But it's true. Bitch even sucked me off in your driveway."

He blew out a soft laugh and rubbed his chin. "This part, I'm sure, was easy. But things are about to get tough for you, my friend."

"Why?" I asked. "Why would they get tough? We had a deal." I felt myself getting pissed. Things were about to change in a way I hadn't agreed to, and I could feel it.

"Relax," Arrow said, holding his hands up in self-defense. "I know we had a deal. And I'll honor that deal. But for now, you need to lay low. Go into hiding."

I stood up, crossed my arms over my chest. "What the fuck for? What did you get me into?"

Arrow stood up in front of me, his six-foot-plus frame dwarfing the hell out of me. "I didn't get you into anything you weren't willing to do. But if Torrin gets wind of the fact that you brought his girlfriend here, he won't be happy."

"Fuck that a-hole," I snapped. "I can handle that twinkie. You tell me when you can hold up to your end of the bargain, get my girl Leigh out here."

Arrow crossed his arms, seemingly pondering that statement. He flicked his head to one side then the other, popping his neck loudly.

"I'll take good care of Leigh. Don't you worry about that. Fuck, if there's one thing I know how to do, it's take care of women. In the meantime," he said, taking a step closer and pointing to the front door, "get your scrawny ass out of my house and somewhere safe unless you want to get yourself killed."

My pulse raced and anger twisted deep inside of me. Arrow wasn't someone I wanted to challenge. I should have thought this through better. I mean, what was between him and Torrin was just that. I shouldn't have injected myself into the bad blood that existed there.

But I sure as shit wouldn't let Torrin Grainger scare me into hiding.

I left Arrow's house without Erin, no fucking clue if they were getting her high or snuffing her out. On the drive home, I told myself to chill the fuck out, that

Arrow would come through. He had always been a man of his word. My brother trusted him with his life and I should do the same. But by the time I got home, I found out everything I had done tonight was all for nothing.

Leigh was there, waiting for me, sitting in the chair by my front door and hugging her legs to her chest.

"What are you doing here, babe?"

She stood up, her eyes a little heavy, serious. "We need to talk."

I knew what she was going to say. I just laughed and shook my head. "You got to be fucking kidding me," I muttered.

"I'm sorry, Jack. But it doesn't matter how hard we try, this just isn't working." She placed her hands on my chest, looked up at me. "You're a good guy. This isn't about that. It's a compatibility thing. Sometimes, it feels like we're trying to force a puzzle piece where it doesn't belong. Or like we're the same sides of two magnets, always pushing against each other."

"Yeah, I get it. You don't have to keep shooting analogies at me." I pulled her hands away, turned my back to her.

All the mistakes I made, getting involved with this cunt, letting her pull out the monster then watching her run scared when she couldn't handle him. I thought Leigh was different. I thought she was the one bitch I could be myself with. Guess I was wrong.

"I don't want to hurt you, Jack."

"Just get the fuck out of here, Leigh."

She placed her hand on my shoulder. "I hope we can still be friends. I know everyone says that, but I mean it."

I spun and laughed in her face. "Why do all you bitches say that shit? Men don't want to be friends with our exes. We just want you to go the fuck away so we can move on to the next."

Her body jerked back, and she wrinkled her face. "Jesus, that's pretty harsh, Jack."

I held my hands up, realizing that by lashing out at her it looked like I gave a fuck, which I didn't. "All I'm saying is, it's no big deal. We're not compatible. I get it. You're off the hook, Leigh. And by the way, thanks for wasting my time."

I barged past her and unlocked my door, feeling the rage build inside me once again. But Leigh had to shoot one more dagger my way.

"I thought I knew you at least a little. Obviously, I didn't. I should have dumped you when I first realized that our relationship was dead."

I whipped around, caught the back of her walking to her car. "It was dead from the get-go, you cunt. You were nothing more than a half-decent lay."

I saw her freeze in her tracks, but I ducked inside my apartment before she could come up with some stupid but witty comeback intended to hurt me.

Fuck her. And fuck Arrow and Torrin. I was done with both those fucking jokers. I didn't need any more negative drama in my life.

Ten

He tells me everything. First, that his name is Arrow Heath. I should have known that even his name would be a weapon.

But then he explains that Jack went to him months ago, wanted him to kidnap me to fulfill a fantasy of mine.

Mine.

That he made Jack bring his arch enemy's girlfriend as payment for the deed.

That Jack admitted she sucked his cock in the driveway of his home.

And that Arrow told Jack to hide so that Torrin wouldn't find him.

I feel sick as he continues. I know that Jack was never good to me, for me, and that he's the reason I've done a complete one-eighty when it comes to how I view myself and men. But that he would go to those lengths to role play some fantasy that, yeah, turned me on when I thought about it but was really his idea, makes me feel so betrayed. On top of all this, I find out that he was really murdered?

"How the fuck did he die? I heard that it was from natural causes."

"I honestly don't know, Leigh. To tell you the truth, I didn't care. I only know that he didn't bother to lay low so it wasn't hard for Torrin to get him. But by the time Torrin realized I had been following you, that I wanted you for my own, it didn't take long for him to figure out you were my weakness. You were the one thing I wanted. So, he decided to take you away from me too."

"You ... followed me? For how long?"

Jesus, I think I feel sicker now.

"About a month. Once I heard Jack was dead, I worried about you. I wasn't sure how close you were, if you were devastated by the news. I watched you come home from work alone each night. And I saw you hanging out with your friend. I could see that you were seemingly unaffected by it all."

"I broke up with him not long after he brought up the fake kidnapping idea. We were a mistake from the beginning."

"Wait. *He* brought up the idea for the kidnapping?"

"Yes. It was his idea."

"You ... didn't want it?"

"Fuck yes, I wanted it. Just not with him."

"Jesus. He really was a shit for brains."

"Well, yes, but forget about him. My question is why would you want Torrin's girlfriend as payment? Because of what he did to your face?"

Arrow growls against my neck. "No. The fucker killed my sister. She was all I had left."

I cringe, squeeze his hand. "Why?"

"Because he's a fucking bastard who only cares about himself. Winslow was only nineteen when he got her pregnant last year. She had gestational diabetes, and he didn't take care of her. Took her out of the country to some remote desert island when she was about seven months along. She had a fucking stroke, died. So did the baby."

"Jesus," I whisper. "I'm sorry."

He hugs me tight, doesn't say anything.

"So, you get Torrin's girlfriend, and I assume you just hold her hostage for a few days. Make him sweat it out? And he decides to get even with *you* by sending someone to attack *me* in the woods?"

Arrow kisses my shoulder, and I turn to look at him.

"No," he answers.

I wait for him to explain, but he's quiet. I feel my body go cold, and my hand slides toward the knife under my pillow. "What did you do, Arrow?"

"I killed her. Well, technically, she killed herself."

I shiver as my fingers wrap around the handle of the blade. Adrenaline begins to surge through my veins. "What do you mean she killed herself?"

"I gave her the tools but she did it. Little combination of heroin and crack. Junkie never knew what hit her."

This is the man who's brought me here. Who kept me locked in a room with a dog bed to sleep on. Who supposedly wants to "keep me safe?"

He's nothing more than a murderer. A heartless killer of innocent women.

I pull in a quick breath and flip over, straddling Arrow with the knife in my hand. I move so quickly he doesn't have time to react as I press the blade to his neck, not far from the bandage where his bullet wound sits. He raises his hands above his head, and a smile starts to spread across his face.

My hands tremble as I try to hold the knife steady. It bobs once when he swallows.

"Go ahead, Leigh. Do it. Then who will look out for you?"

I push against his flesh, but he doesn't flinch. "Victor. Boris."

Arrow chuckles. "Yes. Boris and Victor will look out for you after you kill their boss."

I swallow. He's right. I have the power, though, to slide into his skin, cut out his Adam's apple if I want. He killed an innocent girl, and all in the name of revenge. That's fucked up. So fucked up.

So, why am I struggling now as I look into those evil eyes that seem to be tugging me to him like a magnet?

I pant, feel desire bloom between my legs as I push the knife harder, deeper. A small line of red appears, and Arrow groans, grits his teeth. His erection is suddenly pushing against my ass, straining to be free. The heat builds there, making me weak, and I want him inside of me now.

His hands move slowly to my chest, and he jerks up my bra. He grips my breasts and squeezes them with so much force, the pain spreads through my chest, down my ribs.

My mouth opens. "*Aaaaaaahhhhh,*" I groan, fighting the urge to scream.

His hands move to my throat, gliding up my skin as I open my eyes and stare at him.

Stare at the smile on his face.

My grip loosens on the blade as his fingers constrict around my throat, just below the collar he placed there. My face pulsates with every beat of my heart, and as I feel myself fade, he flips me over on my back, presses his body weight into me as the knife goes falling onto the pillow.

"No," I grumble. "You're a bad person."

He breathes heavy in my face, that goddamn smirk still there. "And yet, the single thing that frightens you is the one thing that makes you want me the most."

I shake my head, roll my hips up to rub my pussy against his hard cock. Why isn't he fucking me yet?

His laughter ripples through me as he tugs the crotch of my underwear aside, slides his fingers through my lips. My belly tightens and I'm sure I'm about to come undone.

"If you don't want me, then why are you so wet?"

"You're a sick fuck," I spit at him, fighting how much I want him.

He dips his head down, sinks his teeth into my neck as his fingers delve deeper inside me. I hold back a moan but can't help pushing my hips against him, pushing those fingers deeper.

"I know. But you want me anyway, and it's driving you crazy."

"You don't know what I want," I say breathlessly.

He pulls his fingers from me, brushes them along my clit, then grips the side of my head with both hands.

"I know exactly what you want. It's *you* who's being resistant."

"I'm being resistant because you don't know what you're doing."

He grumbles out a laugh. My arousal leaks down my slit, wetting the bed below.

"Just give it up already."

"Prove that you know what I want, and I will."

His eyes flicker, and he reaches next to my head for the knife. He slides the sharp edge down the side of my face, his nostrils flaring. I feel his cock bounce against my pussy again, and I can't help but let out a moan. His breathing increases as he circles the tip of the blade around my nipple, making it pucker against the cold, sharp steel.

"Fuck," I whisper, feeling the ache in my belly grow.

I freeze as he continues to drag the knife down my breast, watching my skin dance with goose bumps as he slides over my flesh, pressing harder as he glides over my ribs. He leans down, tugs my nipple into his mouth and sucks gently, groaning deeply. I buck my hips against him, feeling lost in a haze of lust. I grind against his erection, no longer caring that I'm giving up. Now, I need him.

He slips the blade under the seam of my panties, looks me in the eyes, then flicks the knife up, cutting away the material. I pull in a rush of air as he does the same thing to the other side, that hunger blazing in his eyes. my chest rises and falls as he tugs down the waist of his briefs, releasing his erection.

And then he's on top of me, holding the knife against my forehead. The cold steel presses down on me as his crown begins to stretch my opening. I huff, angling my ass up for more.

He tosses the knife aside, caresses my face. "I can't prove that I know what you want without your trust."

I press my palms to his chest, drag my fingertips down his flesh. The nightlight illuminates his good side. the side that isn't covered in scars.

"What do you want?" he asks.

"You," I answer, without hesitating, without remorse.

He pushes inside of me, all the way, and it steals my breath. His lips crash against mine, his tongue searching my mouth as his cock slides in and out of me. I twist my fingers through his hair, kissing him, feeling his growls hit the back of my throat.

He pulls out of me, stands up and tugs down his underwear to the floor, then rakes his nails up my legs. I sit up on my elbows and unbuckle my bra, then toss it aside. Arrow throws my legs out to the side and buries his face in my folds. I feel his tongue dip inside then come out to circle my clit. Fingers plunge deep inside me, massage the front of my walls as I grip the headboard behind me. When I feel the knife, I pick it up, pass it to Arrow.

"Here," I say, still rocking my hips up and down. I don't know what I want him to do with it. I just want him to have it, use it however he wants.

He takes it from my hand. His eyes search mine as he turns the blade to the side, then touches the sharp edge to my labia.

I huff a "yes."

Holding the knife horizontally, he wedges it underneath my clit and lifts up the swollen bud of tissue. Light glints off the metal as he angles it, and when he smooths his tongue in circles over my inflamed tissue, I begin to tremble.

"*Fuuuuuuuck,*" I groan. My ass muscles clench tight, and I'm afraid to thrust for fear of being cut.

I don't like physical pain. But apparently I like the fear of it.

He keeps his eyes on my face as I hold myself up, watching his tongue whip back and forth in small but quick strokes. I realize how easily he could cut his tongue. But watching him hold the knife against my pussy, sharp blade to tender flesh, sends me rocketing over the edge. My body shudders. He growls.

I convulse as he tosses the knife aside and pulls my clit past his lips. My head hits the pillow and I fist his hair as he moves closer, climbs on top of me.

His mouth is on mine, and he's inside me again, moving in deep strokes that take my breath away. I wrap my legs around his hips, he pins my arms above my head. I close my eyes and feel him take me, fill me so full I can't help but come again.

When he comes, he drives deep, grinds against my insides until I'm raw, and until he goes soft. But still, I beg him not to stop.

"I have to," he says. "Can't shoot pool with a noodle."

I laugh, and his lips are on my neck, biting, licking, and sucking, hard.

"Are you giving me a hickey?" I ask, running my hands down the length of his back. His muscles are so hard, they make me hungry for round two.

His lips pop. "Yes"

My skin stings where he was. "Marking your turf?"

"Marking you every time you get switchy with me."

"Switchy?" I ask.

He bites my cheek. "Yes. Switchy."

I giggle. "I have no idea what you're talking about. But if getting switchy earns me a hickey, I may want to do it more."

Arrow brushes my hair out of my face, examines me closely. "That doesn't surprise me."

I trace my fingers over his scars. "Were you afraid to show me what you looked like?"

He blows out a hard breath. "I didn't want to freak you out."

"You didn't think the hood and cape would do that?"

"You liked the disguise. The mystery. It kept you grounded, too. Kept you in line."

Maybe he's right. The fact that I couldn't see his face did earn him a little time with me, an initial sort of respect. But seeing his face wasn't what caused my change of heart.

"I was grounded until those bullets came at us."

Arrow rolls over on his back, pulling me on top of him. I laugh softly. He tucks my hair behind my ears then pushes my head to his chest. "I know it scared you. I don't ever want that to happen again."

I feel his heart bump on my ear. "So, what now? How long do we stay here?"

I run my fingers up his arms, grip his biceps and squeeze.

"We stay here until Torrin is out of the picture. I'm done with him."

What he did to Torrin's girlfriend slams into me, the reality of who I'm with impossible now to ignore. "Out of the picture?" I twist my head up to look at him, resting my chin on my knuckles against his pecs.

He bores his eyes into me. "Yes, Leigh. Out of the picture. I want him dead, and I will not apologize for that." His proclamation seems to have some hostility behind it.

I cup his face. "Okay."

He puts his hand on the back of my head and kisses me with a gentleness that catches me by surprise. I feel like I can't get enough of him. But the reality of our situation, of my situation, comes rushing back far too soon.

I roll off of him, nestle my body against his warmth, more unanswered questions running through my mind. "That was one of Torrin's men who found me on the trail, wasn't it?"

"Yes. Slimy little fuck."

"So, you were both following me at the same time?"

"He was following you. I was following him. And if I hadn't been, he would have killed you."

My stomach rolls. My blood feels like it's curdling. I grit my teeth, surprised at what I'm about to say.

"I want Torrin dead."

A soft grumble erupts from Arrow, interrupting thoughts I've never had before.

"Don't say it if you don't mean it." His body tenses, like he's worried I don't.

"Oh, I fucking mean it."

I hear him pull in a breath as he reaches for my hand, moves it to his cock. It's stiff as a board, hot. And it twitches under my fingers.

"Tell me how you want me to do it," he growls.

I rub his silky hard length, swipe the pre-cum in a slow circle around his crown. "Painfully. And while I fucking watch."

He pulls me on top of him, lifts my ass, and plunges his cock deep inside of me. I collapse on top of his chest as he wraps his arms around me.

"God fucking *damn*," he groans.

My walls tighten around his girth. I'm so turned on, it feels like lava is coursing through my veins, ripping me open from the inside out.

"Oh god, don't stop," I cry, an orgasm threatening to explode from me.

"Never," he growls. "Especially if you keep talking like that."

Something dark blooms inside of me, from a seed that was probably planted years ago, long before I met Arrow. But he's the only one who's made it take root. And I know that what he's planning for Torrin will only make it grow.

I just hope it doesn't grow so big there's not enough water in the world to feed it.

Eleven

When I wake up the next morning, I'm cold to the bone. The covers have been pushed down, and as I roll over to look at Arrow, I see he's lying on his stomach. I've never been with a man that sleeps on his stomach, but I think it shows a confidence. An absence of fear.

His right side is pushed into the pillow, and all I can see are the twisted scars that span his left side. God, he looks so fucked up, yet so fucking sexy all at once. His arms are lying above his head, huge, muscular limbs I want around me right now.

Our bodies feel like worlds apart and I don't like that. I pull the covers back up over me and scoot closer. Heat pours off him and envelops me. This is much better than being on the floor.

As I watch his back rise and fall, I think about him fucking Boobs yesterday, and I wonder how many women are in his life, and does this bother me? I've always been what I consider to be the normal amount of jealous. But I've never been with anyone who cheated on me—other than Jack but that doesn't count at this point—so I never really had those kinds of trust issues. Thinking of him fucking someone else doesn't trigger any sort of negative reaction from me.

But when I hear them call him Master inside my head, it makes my gut twist. Yeah, I definitely don't like that.

I slide my arm across his back and toss a leg over his ass. And since his arms look edible, I sink my teeth into his triceps, sealing my lips to his skin and sucking softly. He tastes like salt and spice, making me heady. He pulls in a deep breath as his eyes flick open.

"Jesus fuck," he mutters, rolling onto his back with the gracefulness of an ox and tucking his hands behind his head. His eyes flip closed again.

"Don't you dare go back to sleep." My hand wanders between his legs. His cock is semi-flaccid, but my touch makes it twitch.

He lies still like he plans to ignore me. I keep stroking him, and his length quickly reaches its full potential. My pussy swells, my heart quickens. His slit is leaking, and I can't help but smirk as I watch his profile.

"Do you have any idea how fucking exhausted I am?"

I snort. "Did someone cut off your balls or something?"

He opens one eye, peeks at me. "What the fuck is *that* supposed to mean?"

"Loosely translated? What kind of man doesn't want morning sex?" I tug his shaft, feel it bounce.

"The kind who was shot yesterday. And still came three times."

My hand freezes. I drop his cock. "Damn, I'm sorry. Don't know what I was thinking."

"I don't know what you were thinking, but I know what I was thinking."

"What's that?"

He licks his lips, pauses briefly. "That you're really fucking gullible."

His body rolls on top of me lightning fast, but, once again, with all the gracefulness of an ox. As a result, my left arm gets crushed between us, and my hair gets wedged between his elbow and the mattress. I think a piece of my scalp is now missing. I end up scream-laughing, but he pushes up on one arm and releases me from my prison of momentary pain.

"You're a dick!" I laugh, slapping his chest with open palms.

He's grinning wide at me, raises his eyebrows, and grips his cock with his free hand. "And you're a bratty little cunt who needs to learn proper morning etiquette."

I roll my eyes. "Please. I know etiquette as well as the next girl."

"That may be the problem." He pushes past my folds, placing his hands on the top of my head as his weight crushes down on me.

Air escapes my lungs in a long moan as he stretches me wide.

"Jesus …. Arrow…"

I flip my legs around his waist, snake my fingers through his dark hair, hook my ankles together as I rock with him. He goes deep, fills me completely. I get lost, tangled up in what he does to me. I let my hands run down his back, grip the swell of his ass as he pumps and grinds.

He growls as my orgasm builds. My walls clamp around him as I crest that ridge. I lift my head up and bury my nose in his neck so I can smell him while I come. Air escapes my lungs in ragged breaths.

I grip the headboard and arch my back. Arrow pushes up on both hands and, still moving his cock in and out of me, lowers his lips to my nipples. His teeth press down, sharp as they bite into my flesh. I let out a cry and push on his chest.

He lifts, looks at me, laughs.

"Fucker," I grumble.

He pulls a face, sits up, grabs my hips. "Oh really?" he says. One hand brushes some of his hair back.

I lift my legs up, set them on his shoulders for a moment. "Bite me again, see what happens."

He smirks and wraps his hands around my ankles. "Challenge accepted."

After turning his head to the side, he places his mouth on my lower leg and sinks his teeth into my Achilles. He then flicks his gaze to watch my face and is quickly rewarded with a look of pain that's stretching my mouth wide open.

"*Aaaahhh!*" I scream, jerking my leg as hard as I can. He holds his arms up, worried I will kick him I guess.

In seconds, I've pushed myself up to a seated position and grabbed him by the wrists. He feigns a surprised look, his cock still hard and pointed to the ceiling. "What are you going to do, little ninja?"

"Oh, you're real funny," I chuckle. My tendon is still throbbing and it's time for a payback.

I shift my weight a little, then give him a hard shove that sends him falling to floor where I land on top of him.

He grunts, but it's followed by laughter. "You little bitch."

I straddle his waist, pin his arms to the floor. "Yeah, but I'm a little bitch that's about to have you by the balls."

His chest is heaving, and his face is stretched into a smile. And I know he's letting me stay up here. He could so pin my ass if he wanted. But I think he kind of likes this, likes me on top.

Just then, Victor barges in the room. "Is everything okay—"

He freezes when he sees us on the floor, both of us unclothed. Arrow twists his head like a contortionist in his direction, and Victor just slowly closes the door back, muttering a "sorry."

I wiggle my ass down as Arrow turns his attention to me again. His dick bobs against the crack of my ass, and I let it brush against my pussy as I maneuver lower and put my head between his legs. I grip the base of him, feel how hard and big he is.

"I can use my mouth, too. But for much better things than biting."

"Mmmm," he groans, gripping my long hair in both his hands. "I know you can use that mouth for better things."

I lower my lips to his cock, lick the underside as I watch him. His eyes narrow, then flair as I show my teeth, graze them along his silky flesh.

"Fuck, Leigh...." he whispers.

I wrap my lips around the circumference and hear him groan as he tugs my hair. Not too hard. Just enough to remind me I better watch myself. But I don't want to bite him back. Not now. I like the way he tastes, the way his thick, salty fluid drizzles on my tongue as I work my mouth over his length. I take him further down with each pass, feeling the head of his cock rub against my tonsils.

I grope his balls, feeling them draw together as I bob my head. His thighs tense and I hear him huff as his dick grows and throbs on my tongue. I squeeze his testicles, easy at first, then increasing the pressure slowly until I hear him whisper, "*ssshhhhhhit....*"

He turns to steel right before hot, earthy liquid pulses on my tongue. I increase the pressure on his sac and he growls before shoving my face down hard on his length. My nose brushes against his flesh.

I release his balls and let my hands roam up his abs, to his chest. I suck as hard as I can, tugging out the last few remnants of his cum. His fingers release my hair, but I don't stop. In fact, I suck him harder. And then those fingers move up my arms, nails raking the surface of my skin. I tingle all over as he softens inside my mouth.

I release him and keep my head down, stick out my tongue, trail it up the front of him, licking his flesh until I get to his chest. His hands press down on my ass, grip my hips, and his nails dig into my flesh as I sweep the tip of my tongue up his chin and to his lips.

He whips his hands up to my head and catches the back of it, pulling me in for a kiss. Groans fill my ears, both soft and loud, hungry and fulfilled, animalistic and gentle. I can't distinguish his from mine.

I think we may have a dangerous sort of chemistry that makes me feel safe for the first time ever. And I've become instantly addicted.

I pull my hair into a ponytail as Arrow comes back in his room. A dark towel is wrapped around his waist, and water speckles his body like dew.

"What are the chances of me getting some new clothes?" I ask, holding my shirt to my nose for a quick sniff test.

"Oh shit," he answers. After lifting his bag onto the bed, he rummages inside and removes a pair of jeans and a cotton top. "I completely forgot I grabbed these before we left my house yesterday. They're clean, too. Never worn."

"Great. First, you forget to tell me you have my phone, and now you withhold clothing?"

Arrow climbs on the bed, and I slowly lower my back to the mattress as he mounts me. "First," he says. "Yesterday was a little fucking nuts, so forgive me for neglecting to remember I brought you a change of clothes."

"You're forgiven," I tell him, dragging the tips of my fingers down his chest.

"And secondly, you'll get your phone and your battery back once I know you're safe." He plants a kiss on my forehead and gets back up.

"My battery? Why do you have my battery?"

"Took it out so your phone couldn't be tracked."

I blow out a breath, flap my lips together, then pick up the stretchy jeans to step into them, femininely commando. Oh well, underwear is overrated. And amazingly, they fit like a glove.

"I'm sending Victor out for breakfast. What do you want?"

"We don't have anything here?" I ask.

Arrow shrugs. "It's my buddy's house. He's out of town, and I don't want to eat up his food."

"Oh. Well, why don't we all go out and get something?"

"Not an option," he says, tugging a shirt over his head. "We're on your home turf, so going out in public isn't a good idea."

I make a face and put my shirt on. "And we're just going to sit here indefinitely?"

"No. I have a plan that will get us out of here and back to my house in a few days." I watch his face light up as he talks about going home. I can't blame him. I know the feeling.

"And, what about getting me back to my house?"

Arrow's face loosens, and I can tell he's about to say something. But a knock at the door interrupts us.

"Yeah?" he calls out.

Victor carefully pokes his head through a crack in the door, in a very PTSD kind of way, and darts his gaze between me and Arrow. "Sorry to intrude. I'm going to get breakfast. Any special requests?"

Arrow looks at me.

"Anything is fine, Victor. I'm not picky," I tell him.

"Boss?"

Arrow pulls his wallet out of his back pocket. "Double what I usually get. Thanks."

"So when do I get to hear about this plan of yours?" I ask him once Victor is out of sight.

He chuckles. "You want all the gory details, don't you? And you called *me* a sick fuck?"

"I haven't asked for any gory details. But I have requested to watch, and that won't change. As a matter of fact, I want to help."

I stand up and walk to Arrow as he buttons his jeans. I reach up to rake my fingers through his damp hair, but he grabs me by the wrist.

"While the thought of that is an erection inducer, I'm not sure it's something I will permit."

I glance at his hand around my wrist. He's trying to re-establish dominance here. I don't mind letting him have it, most of the time. But I'm done letting other men make decisions for me.

"I'm not one of your slaves, Arrow." I pull my arm away from his grasp, and his stunned look makes me wonder if he was even aware that he grabbed me. "I know that you don't want me to get hurt. But I won't stand off on the sidelines without us having a discussion about it."

He narrows his eyes, searches my face with a conflicted stare. Finally, he says, "I make the final decision. And what I say goes, Leigh. It's non-negotiable."

"Naturally," I answer.

I have to lie, tell him I'll agree to whatever he decides. But if he doesn't give me the answer I want, I'll change his mind because everything is negotiable. *Everything*.

"Glad we agree on something. But this time, I don't want you going back on your word."

I tilt my head and lift a brow. "*This* time?"

After placing his palms on my cheeks, he tilts his head back at me. "You made me a promise yesterday."

"What did I promise?" Shit, I have no idea what he's talking about.

"That if I explained why you were here, you would call me Master."

Our conversation in the basement yesterday floats back up to the surface. "As my recollection serves, I merely said I wouldn't call you Master until I knew who was trying to kill me and why. I never said that I would do so right away."

I give him a wink, but I don't think he appreciates it.

"How did I not anticipate that you would come up with some sort of loophole?"

I shrug at him, place my hand over his, and pull it to my lips for a kiss. "I honestly don't know. I'm kind of surprised with it myself."

The truth is, I have changed in the few days I've been here. Changed for the better. I can feel it. I'm not the same girl I was when I was on the Butte Trail several nights ago. So the fact that I'm digging in my heels and not kowtowing to his demands is a little new for me, too.

His hands fall away from my head. And I'm suddenly terrified that he's disappointed in me.

"Well, I can't say that I'm not disappointed." *Great...* "But I also have only myself to blame."

His words jar me. As he turns his back to me, I feel like I've suddenly become the enemy. "You make it sound as though having a strong woman around is criminal."

Arrow steps into his boots as I wait for a response. "It's not criminal." He finishes tying his boots and turns to me once again. "But I know what I want."

I lift my eyes, feel my heart hammer. "And that's a woman who will address you by some label you have preconceived notions about?"

"No." He runs his teeth over his bottom lip. Flicks his gaze down my body, hugs my waist with his strong hands. "What I want is a woman who will let me take care of her and who knows her place with me."

"Not all women want to be taken care of."

"I get that," he says, pulling me closer to him. "And those women are not for me."

I stare into his eyes, looking more brown today than green, and I grit my teeth together as I think of something clever to say. But I'm stumped. And if I'm being honest, a little stung, especially when I consider the crazy amount of passion we seem to share.

"Not even if you're compatible in the bedroom?"

The corner of his mouth lifts, and he presses his lips to mine. His tongue darts in and out in a flash, forcing hot desire to spread between my legs. I push my hands up his chest, remembering what that tongue did down there just a few hours ago.

"Compatibility in the bedroom has its place. And I've always kept those women around."

"Oh? Like *Boobs*? Or the other woman at your house whom you allowed to sleep in your bed?"

"Yes," he says, brushing his thumb along my lips.

My body tingles.

"And the women you don't have compatibility in the bedroom with, like the one who challenged you that night. What happens to them?"

"They've always had a place, too. Monique was very subservient. She gave amazing back massages, made my coffee for me every morning and made sure that my clothes were washed, pressed, and ready for me. She was perfect in every way. Except that she wanted a part of me I wasn't willing to give."

"Then why did you get so angry with her, when all she wanted was to share your bed?"

Arrow's jaw tightens, and he turns from me. "Sometimes I lose my temper. It's not something I'm proud of."

He raises his arms, runs his hands through his hair. And I don't know how he will react this time, but I need to touch him, feel his skin on mine. I wrap my arms around his waist, press the side of my head to his back. "Your temper doesn't scare me. It ... it turns me on."

I feel him react. His head turns in my direction, and he pries my arms off him, spinning to face me. He stares at me for a moment, then closes his eyes as he pulls in a tight breath. "I know it does, Leigh. And that makes things so much more complicated."

"Complicated? How?"

He lowers his forehead to mine, brushes his thumbs over my breasts. My nipples tingle and curl up tight. "Because, it makes me want you in a way I've never wanted anyone. And you're hesitant to kneel at my feet."

His voice is filled with more heartfelt emotion than I ever would have expected. It makes my chest feel like it's opening and a river is pouring through it. "I've never done anything like that, Arrow. It's just ... foreign to me. Why can't two people just be together, without expectations? Without demands? Without conforming to labels?"

He looks to the side, and I wonder if what I've said is getting through. It's not that I don't want to kneel for him. I just don't want to force myself to fit inside of a mold to please someone else. And why is this even an issue? I don't really know Arrow, except that he's capable of killing innocent people. What the hell am I thinking, getting involved with someone like this? Why the fuck am I considering kneeling for a murderer?

Fuck, I know why. Those same traits that make me question why I want him are the same ones that make me want him. I love how he scares me. I love how dangerous he is. And Arrow is the only man who doesn't just know where my buttons are, he knows exactly how to push them. How can I not want that?

He doesn't answer my question. And I have to believe it's because he doesn't have an answer. Maybe he wants to feel that same freedom that comes with shedding expectations. The freedom from being the same person you've been your whole fucking life that got you nowhere.

"Let's go get some coffee while we wait on breakfast."

"Sure. Just one thing."

He looks at me as he opens the door. "Yeah?"

"I'm not eating on the floor."

I brush past him, holding back the smirk. His hand thwacks my bottom but I keep on walking. At least he doesn't seem to be pushing the envelope. It's hard to believe that just 24 hours ago he was still wearing that damn cape and hood. And I can't help but wonder what the next 24 hours will hold.

Twelve

And you're sure Torrin and his men haven't been by my house?"

Victor wipes his mouth with a napkin. "I'm telling you that Monte and Wyatt have been posted there since right after the incident yesterday. According to them, no one has returned. No one has driven past. No one has so much as coughed in their direction, boss."

I listen to Arrow and Victor go back and forth as Boris and I sit and eat.

"I want to go back, then. Get a few things. From there, we'll move to the next step, what we discussed yesterday."

Victor nods. "When would you like to do this?"

Arrow glances at me, as if I'm part of the answer. I take a sip of coffee and hold his gaze.

"The sooner the better. After breakfast is as good a time as any."

"And do you still want to get Leigh to Trinity's?"

"Get me to where?" I ask, setting my mug down.

Arrow makes a face and presses his fingers to his temple. "I haven't had a chance to talk with her about it yet, so no."

"Who the fuck is Trinity?" I can already see myself wanting to become explosive over this. "And why would I go to her?"

Victor tries to interject, and Arrow presses two fingers to the bridge of his nose.

"She is no one, *fetita*. She is … *was* … someone we believe can keep you safe while boss wraps up a few loose ends."

"Oh. Are you fucking her, too?" I ask Arrow.

He bursts into laughter as Victor crumples his sandwich wrapper and leaves the table. Boris just darts his gaze between the two of us, lifting his eyes like Arrow and I are suddenly a spectator sport.

"I'm not sure if anyone is fucking Trinity," Arrow replies. "I imagine her pussy to be a circle of claws, additionally surrounded by razor-edged teeth."

Boris lets out a laugh and gets up from the table. "That's my cue."

"Sorry, man." Arrow watches Boris disappear, a smirk on his face. "I think he has a thing for her."

"Razor-edged teeth? Now I want to go." I rest my chin on folded hands as I bat my eyes. "Seriously. She sounds vicious. I'd like to meet her."

He shakes his head and pushes his plate aside. "The swan is nothing like you think she is. Trust me, Leigh."

"The swan?" I ask.

"I mean Trinity. She goes by the swan. Whatever. I'm not sure that hiding out at her place is the best idea, though."

"Why is that?" Not that I want to hide anywhere without Arrow, but still.

He shakes his head, clasps his fingers together. "I've known her for fifteen years, since I was about twenty. She's sent us some jobs here and there. But to be honest, I have no idea who's coming and going from her place. She could be allies with my enemies. I just don't know."

"She sends you jobs? Are you talking ...?" I mimic slicing my throat, and Arrow nods.

I'm reminded again of just how little I know about this man.

"Come on. I want to get out of here, head to my house. We can talk on the way."

I get the feeling that Arrow is suddenly uncomfortable here, though I don't know why. But by the time we get in his car, I can tell he's relaxed somewhat.

"Which one are you having trouble with?"

He shoots a look my way. "Huh?"

"Boris or Victor? Which one?"

He flicks me an odd look as we pull out of the driveway. "That's not what's going on. I trust them both with my life."

"Then why the rush to leave?"

He tightens his grip on the steering wheel. Shifts in his seat. "I just wanted you alone for a few minutes. I'm ... constantly surrounded by people. By men."

I feel a warmth flow through my veins as he flicks his gaze at me. It's the first time he's made me feel like he wants me for me.

"You've been surrounded by women, too."

Arrow blows out a soft laugh. "I suppose you're right. But none like you."

I smile. "I'll take that as a compliment." I'm not sure if he meant it that way, but it feels like he did. "Where did you find all your womens, by the way?"

He hesitates. "Friends of friends."

I snicker. "Okay. Fair enough."

We ride silently for a few minutes, and I think about how I've gone from having no control to feeling like I've got more than ever before. How did this happen?

Because I stood up to a man who has more power than anyone I've ever known.

"What do you think made you this way?" I ask him, suddenly curious about the history of the man under the cape.

He gives me an odd look. "You mean why am I an asshole?"

"I didn't say that at all. Wasn't even thinking it. I meant the whole dom thing."

"I don't like to think of myself as a dom." He shudders, and I can't help but laugh.

"Too many negative connotations?"

"I don't like being labeled. I guess you and I are similar in that sense. I'm just … me. And yes, I like to be in charge, take the lead. So, why am I like that, you ask?"

He curls his gaze at me and I nod.

"My first girlfriend when I was in college used to call me master, more as a joke because I was always…" He pauses, like he's searching for the right word.

"Telling her what to do?" I finish.

"Ha ha ha," he says, shooting me a full-finger fuck you. "No. Well, yeah. I probably was. But mostly it was good advice. Like, don't fucking walk around campus after dark without calling me or one of your friends. Or, make sure you eat breakfast before your final exams. Shit I know she was bad about doing. She needed me to take care of her, and I wanted to take care of her like that."

"That would drive me batshit."

"Well. Maybe you need to be told different things. Like, don't walk through the woods alone at night."

I glare at him and he flashes me a smug smile. I stick my tongue out at him while he isn't looking.

But damn it, I know he's right. If I'm being honest, there have been many times I needed someone to steer me away from bad decisions, Jack being one of those bad decisions. If I'd had someone to grab me by the shoulders and say, *don't do that shit!*, I wouldn't have gotten myself into this whole mess. I'd probably be sitting at home right now, enjoying a mushroom pizza and a glass of wine. Not being chauffeured around by someone trying to keep me from being killed.

"Wait a minute," I say, rubbing my head. "You say you like taking care of women?"

"Yeah. I do, why?"

"Well, earlier you were talking about how subservient one of your girls was. Saying that she gave massages and made your coffee, washed your clothes. So you like being taken care of, too."

"Of course I like to be taken care of. But my girls take care of me in little ways. Things that save me time, trouble. Not by ensuring that I'm safe, healthy, and emotionally stable ... happy."

For some reason, I think about the collar around my neck when he says that. I've almost forgotten about it. Which is kind of funny given how much I hated it when it first went on.

"So what was with the leash? You get off on that? Or does it fall into the category of providing emotional stability?"

He looks at me, flicks his gaze toward my chest. Ignoring my sarcasm, he says, "Yeah, I get off on it. The same girlfriend that called me master wore a collar and leash long before it was a *thing*. I thought you might like it, too."

I wrinkle my forehead at him, wondering why he would even remotely think that. He must be reading my mind because he shoots me a look.

"Don't forget it was *your* boyfriend who said you wanted this, Leigh. I had no idea you two had broken up before he was killed, or that it was mostly his idea."

Shit, I hadn't thought of that. His statement is like an epiphany. Or more like a slap to the face. He took me from the woods, assuming that I had a kidnap fantasy because of what Jack had told him. And even though I liked entertaining the idea, that fantasy would have never entered my mind.

"Damn," I mutter. "You're right. You must have thought I was getting off on all of it."

He shrugs. "Not really. But I was. And, I mistakenly assumed that since we stopped that fucker from raping you, that you would trust me."

My stomach turns sour, and I can feel the blood drain all the way down to my toes. I rest my head against the cool glass and hug my waist. Arrow glances my way, places his hand on my leg.

"Shit, I'm sorry," he says. "Guess I shouldn't have phrased it like that."

I pull in a deep breath, feeling myself get shaky as I recall that night, the way he pushed me against that tree, the sound of his voice, the way he smelled. The look on his face before Arrow cut him ear to ear. I've been pushing the whole thing down, shoving it as deep as it will go. But hearing him acknowledge it out loud shakes me to my core.

"No, it's ... I need to deal with it."

His hand grips my leg, and I gravitate to it, resting my palm on top. I lace my fingers through his, feeling my sweat mix with his. He squeezes, reminding me he's here. Not going anywhere.

"I'm not the person you thought I was," I tell him. "I'm not the girl who will fall at your feet, beg you to let her sleep in your bed, or ask to be led around on a leash."

"I know that," he answers, his voice low, but understanding.

I twist in the seat to face him, keeping a firm grip on his hand. "Yesterday, you said I belonged to you. You were *adamant*." My heart pounds as he looks at me with astonishment in his eyes before moving his gaze back to the road. "You pulled me to you, slammed my body to yours as if you were staking your claim and never wanted to let me go." His eyes widen as I continue. "I just wonder if that possessiveness is just as strong now as before."

Arrow pulls his hand from me, hits the brakes, and turns the steering wheel to the right. The car rumbles to a stop along the shoulder of the highway. I throw my hands on the dash to keep from flying forward. The tires grind along the gravel as we go from sixty to zero in a flash.

"Jesus *fuck*!" I screech. "Have you lost your mind?"

Arrow slams the car in park and turns to face me. He grips the side of my head, pulls my face to his, a fury in his eyes I've never witnessed in anyone.

"Let me be crystal fucking clear," he grumbles. I can see the anger written in the creases of his face. "I don't do take-backsies." His nostrils flair, and I tremble. "When I stake my claim, that shit is for good."

I draw a few shaky breaths, think about our conversation in his bedroom an hour ago. "But, just a little while ago, you said you wanted a certain type of woman. A woman who would let you take care of her. A *subservient* woman."

His scar side twitches. He licks his lips, traces his tongue along the ridge as he looks at my mouth. "You may not want to hear this, Leigh, but you're more subservient than you're willing to admit."

I look at my reflection in his eyes, see the face staring back at me, and it's the face of a stranger. I don't know who I am anymore. I'm clinging to the belief that strength is what keeps me going. But the truth is, I don't know if that strength is mine or if it's borrowed. I don't know what's mine at all anymore.

"I am not subservient." Tears scorch my eyes, spill over, run down my cheeks, two, three at a time.

Arrow's face softens in sympathy. He bumps his forehead to mine, and I don't know why I'm crying at all, but my tears quickly vanish as he licks my face from bottom to top, erasing my sorrow as if it never existed.

I run my fingers over his as they remain fisted in my hair. His tongue navigates to my mouth, and he kisses me. A line of cars roar past us on the freeway, the resulting cross wind slamming into us with a shocking force that scares me.

"We should leave," I whisper, moving my hands to his face.

Brushing his thumbs along my lips, he swipes away his saliva. "I want to fuck you right now."

I laugh, eyes closed, feel the heat build. "Take me home, then."

But I'm not talking about my home. And it's then I realize I'm already feeling like I belong to him.

His eyes flicker and I hear a soft rumble in his throat. That energy swirls around us. It's palpable. It's poisoning. It's instantly addictive. I slide my hand up his scars, cover them with my palm. Not trying to hide them but wanting to feel just a little of his pain.

He puts the car in drive and starts inching forward, merges on the highway. I watch him, every now and then turning my attention back to him, needing to drink him up.

It takes another thirty minutes to get to his house. Arrow swears under his breath when he sees a car in the driveway.

"That's not him, is it?"

"Torrin? No. It's one of the girls." My gut tightens. "One I'd rather not deal with right now."

But as soon as he pulls up next to her Hyundai, he's forced to deal with her on the spot. She comes out of the house, several bags slung over her shoulder. It's one of the women from the other night. The one he let sleep with him. Before he can get out of the car, she approaches the driver's side, leans down.

He lowers the window and her head pops through, flicking her gaze between me and Arrow for a second. "I know I should go about this in a different way, but things have gotten a little too intense for me. I'm getting out."

Arrow turns off the engine, gets out of the car, pulls her aside. His window is still down, so I can hear what he's saying to her.

"You shouldn't have come back here without telling me. You could have gotten hurt."

I can see her hands move up to his chest. But I can't see her face, or his.

"I know. But I just wanted to get it over with. I … um … left the collar on your bathroom counter. And here's your key."

His hands move down to her waist. He pulls her into a hug. "Okay. I'm sorry about everything. I shouldn't have put you in this position." There's a pause, and I have to look away.

"I knew what I was getting into. Take care of yourself. And… take care of *her*."

I don't know if she's referring to me, but I have to admit that my jealousy dissipates when she says that. I chew on the inside of my lip, and when I hear her car door close, I see Arrow appear on my side. He opens the door.

"I only have to get a few things, but I don't want to leave you out here."

"Yeah, sure," I answer, following him to the house. I watch the woman drive off. She keeps her eyes on me until she's out of sight.

Once we're inside, he flips three bolts, putting his house on lockdown.

I follow him up the winding staircase and to the room with the walk-in closet. He makes a beeline for the dresser at the end of the room. "Make yourself comfy. I have a few things to pack."

I take off my jacket and sit on the bed. And he proceeds to pull out wads of shirts, socks, underwear, I don't know what all is there. My gaze floats around the room as he walks to the closet. He comes out seconds later with a small suitcase, starts tossing things inside. I peek inside, see the long row of clothes I went through the other day.

"Quick question."

"Yes?"

He walks back the closet, comes out with his hooded cape. My insides ripple like jelly as he folds it up, watching me.

"Why do you have so many women's clothes in your closet?"

He smirks. "I'm not a cross-dresser, if that's what you're getting at."

"Wouldn't think of suggesting it."

"They're for anyone who wants them. Including you. Would you like another go?" He waves his hand toward the door, inviting me to go inside.

"No thanks. Are you going back to your friend's house after this?"

He shifts his gaze down to me as he tucks the cape carefully on top of his layer of clothes. "Yes. And you are too. With me."

"And then what?"

He flips the top of the suitcase down, zips it shut, clasps his hands behind his head. "Victor is working on narrowing down Torrin's location. Once he does, I'm going after him, getting him on his own turf, the same fucking way he did me."

"You're going to kill him at his house?"

His jaw ticks. "Not his house, no. His fucking hideout. His *safehouse*. His home would be too easy. Fuck that shit. I've got a message to send."

"And you don't know where his hideout is?"

"No. That's the one thing we've always left alone, the one line we wouldn't cross. But that mother fucker crossed the line for the last time with me. And I'm ending that shit right now."

His face darkens when he talks about killing Torrin in the one place he feels safe. A dichotomy of sickness and desire ripples through me as I observe that dark curtain fall around him. But he's no longer interested in talking, it seems.

He walks over, kneels on the floor in front of me. He pries my legs open, courses his fingers up my legs. I swallow hard, feeling the damp heat push through the seam of my jeans.

I run my fingers through his dark hair as he presses his nose to my crotch and pulls in a deep breath. He opens his mouth, clamps his teeth around my mound. I thrust and hold my hips in place, staring at the imperfections of his perfect face. Then I fall back on the bed, sinking in as Arrow grinds his face in my heat, biting and blowing hot breath through the fabric.

"Shit," I murmur. "I think I could come, you keep that up."

He flips to the inside of my thigh and bites hard enough to make me lurch back to a sitting position. I try to push his head away, but he's like solid steel as he returns to the "V" between my legs, parts his lips, grazes his teeth along the denim.

I grind and groan, feeling him rub against my clit. He watches me, quickly drags his tongue along the stitching, makes me purr.

"Oh fuck…"

My palms sweat, my heart thuds, skips around. His hands reach up, fist my breasts. I cover them and close my eyes as my stomach tightens. His mouth sends me closer to bliss, white teeth scratching the material as it presses against my swollen bump. And when he clamps down in soft pulses, an orgasm rockets through me in violent pulsations.

I fall back again, and Arrow lifts my feet off the floor, setting them on the top of the mattress as he rubs his mouth hard against my pussy. I huff as my body shudders uncontrollably.

He crawls on the bed, pinches the bottom of my shirt between his teeth and pulls it up. He covers my stomach in kisses, making my nipples tighten. I clamp my legs around his waist as he makes his way up, grinning at me like he's the shit and he knows it.

"You're ruining me, you know that?"

His hands press down my hair, breath hits my cheek. "You're already ruined. Admit it."

I let out a feminine growl because I know he's right. "I hate you."

Chuckling, he straddles me, massages my breasts, looks straight into my eyes. "I hate you too, Leigh."

I paint his body with my gaze, waiting for more. But more doesn't come when he flips his leg back over the edge of the bed and leaves me alone with the fading remnants of a good orgasm. Ok, great.

"I want to stay here with you," I tell him, tugging my jeans from between my pussy lips and rolling to my side.

He's already at the closet again, pulling out a pair of boots to change into. "We can't stay here. I have to get back and strategize with Victor."

I pull a face. "You do realize there's this little thing called a phone. Hell, you can even use your phone's camera and skype. Or facetime, whatever."

"It's not the same thing as doing it in person." He scrunches his face then gives me an understanding look. "I want to stay here, too. Fuck, you think I like being away from my own house?"

"Then don't leave," I tell him, crawling across the bed that I really fucking want to share with him tonight. "Let's take your car into town, get a cab back, make the place look vacant in case Torrin shows."

Blowing out a hard breath, Arrow doesn't seem to share my point of view. "If I was going to consider this, and believe me, that's a big *if*, there's no fucking way I'd leave us stranded here without a car."

I lift my face to him. "So, you are considering it?"

"Not really, no."

I wrinkle my face. "But you could be persuaded."

He tilts his head to the side, crosses his arms over his chest, closes his scarred eye. "Persuade me. I dare you."

I can't help but smile. I always did like a challenge. But how the fuck can I persuade him? What do I have to bargain? Fucker already has my pussy. He knows that.

There is one thing he wants from me. I think he's made that pretty clear. But would he be happy with a temporary fix?

I get up on my knees, bury my nose in his neck, take in his scent. He grazes the tips of his fingers down my back and laughs softly.

"I definitely like your style."

"Let's stay here, wait on Torrin together, and I'll give you something you want."

He tugs my hair and looks me in the eye. "Before I ask what, explain to me why you want to stay here so much."

That's a good question. One I'm not sure I can easily answer. I just know how suddenly right it feels to be here. And I think part of me wants to feel like we're a team, the two of us taking on the shitstorms of the world.

"Maybe it brings me comfort when I can't be at my own place. I'm not sure. I just don't want to leave." I trail his scars with my finger as his eyes dart around my face.

"Okay. So what will you give me?"

I smile. "One night as your property, Master."

His eyes flicker as his nails dig into my flesh.

"Whatever you want, at your feet or on the floor."

I spread open his shirt, flick the groove of his neck with the tip of my tongue. A husky groan comes up from this throat. "Now you're speaking my language."

I sink my teeth into his flesh, images flashing in my mind of him taking me right here. But now it's up to him.

"So that's a yes?"

When he grips my ass and tugs me close, and I feel the heat of his erection, I know what his answer will be.

He reaches up and cups my breasts, moaning into my hair. "Let me make a few phone calls."

I watch him walk out of the room, and I can't help but smile. Arrow may be the size of a bulldozer, but he's nothing more than a malleable teddy bear.

Thirteen

Victor's setting the stage now. He's got four of my men hovering in the shadows of Torrin as we speak."

"Where is he?"

"Last I heard, he was leaving his sister's house and headed toward his own place."

"So they'll see if he comes here. That's good."

"Yeah. Except it will ruin my plans to get him when he least expects it."

"That's really important to you, huh?"

"Damn fucking important."

I don't try to argue with Arrow. I'm actually on his side. I can relate to that feeling of wanting to take his ass down on his own terms. It's what I want, too.

I snuggle up on the sofa next to him, enjoying the fire but a little surprised he doesn't already have me on the floor in front of him. I'm basically waiting for him to implement what I promised him.

And as I take in the eloquence of this room, and his whole house, I start to wonder where he got the money for such luxuries when he obviously doesn't punch a time clock.

"Truth or dare," I tell him.

He chuckles. "Okay."

"What do you do for work when you're not plotting your revenge on Torrin?"

"Ah, I knew this question would come one day."

"Is it a bad question?"

"Not at all."

"Oh, well, I have a million more questions to ask you, so get ready."

"And I might have answers, I might not. We'll see. To answer your first question, I used to work as a private investigator. But five years ago, my father died. I got most of his estate since Winslow was still a minor."

"Really? So you grew up here, in this house?"

"No. I bought this house once the estate paid, about four years ago. I've been doing upgrades ever since. The bedroom upstairs used to be my dungeon, but I've just turned it into the master suite. The room you were in was my sister's, before she died."

I cringe as he continues.

"And I have plans to build onto the home, make it even bigger for the kids I hope to have someday."

"You want kids?" I angle my gaze up at him. He looks somewhat forlorn.

"Yes. I'd love to have a family, little rug rats running around."

Picturing Arrow with a baby just amps up the hotness factor for me. There are few things sexier than a big, strong, nurturing dad.

"What about you?" he asks.

Feeling a little put on the spot, I don't know how to answer. I've never given a lot of thought to having kids, but maybe because I never met the right person.

"I'll take whatever life gives me. I don't think we can do any more than that, right?"

"I think we can always do more than that. You have choices, Leigh."

"Yes, I know I have choices. But sometimes life makes certain choices for us."

He runs his hand through my hair, gives me a sympathetic look. "Why do I get the feeling that you're speaking about something very specific?"

I laugh softly. "Well, it was you who rescued me in the woods almost a week ago."

"True, but that statement had years of pain underneath it."

Years of pain. He's got that right.

"Tell me about your family," he asks, lowering his voice, as if he knows.

"You *know* about my family," I say, remembering him holding up my phone yesterday.

"I don't know what happened," he says. "Or how it affected you."

"Okay, well, the abridged version is that my mom was unreliable. Enjoyed partying more than parenting, so most of that fell on my dad. She left for good when I was a teen. Right on the cusp of adolescence and when I needed her the most."

"Shit, I'm sorry. Was your dad good to you?"

"Yeah, he was the best. He was cuddly and loving and fucking did everything for me. Unfortunately, he also smoked himself right into lung cancer. Died when I was twenty-one."

He pulls me close and kisses the top of my head. "Sounds like we both lost. Though my mom was at least there for me before she died."

"How did yours die?"

"Mom, early onset dementia and my dad in a car accident. He was healthy as a fucking horse. It sucked when he left. And I'd give every penny to have him back."

"I'd give anything to have my dad back," I murmur.

Arrow pulls me tightly to him. "How did we get on such a morbid subject?"

"Me," I answer, laughing. "And now it's up to me to get us past it." I sit up on the couch and straddle Arrow's lap, brushing his hair back and holding it down on his scalp. He beams a smile up at me. "You haven't told me what you wanted from me yet. I'm in limbo. And when I go in limbo, my mind starts to wander."

Arrow cups my face, slides his fingers through my hair and fists it tightly. "I'm aware. And that's about to change right now."

"How so?" I ask, looking at his full lips.

"Wait here and I'll show you."

He stands up and turns around before setting me back down on the sofa. When he disappears, I pull the soft blanket up over me. I enjoy the crackle of the fire, the soft light spilling out on the floor. For the first time in days, I don't have a single worry.

I glance up at the books on the shelf. Suddenly curious, I get up and make my way across the room. I see rows and shelves of leather-bound books, encyclopedias, and what looks to be antique book ends and candle holders. I wonder if they belonged to his mother and father or if he just has a thing for old books.

When Arrow appears in the doorway, his shadow looms ahead of him, and for an instant, I think I'm seeing things.

He's holding a piece of rope, circular in his grip as he approaches me. And I immediately notice he's removed the bandage from his neck and replaced it with a series of smaller band-aids. He stops in front of me, wraps the rope around my neck, and secures it with a knot. His expression is hard as he looks at me.

I think he's going to tell me something, give me instructions. But he simply turns around and leads me up the winding staircase.

When I walk in, I see he's lit the candles, making it look as though the small trees next to his bed are on fire. The shadows of the flames lick the walls.

He walks in front of me and focuses his attention on my clothes, starting with unbuttoning my jeans. He tugs them down my waist, giving them a hard jerk until they're below the swell of my cheeks. He touches my flesh, the tips of his large fingers making my skin tingle with electricity. His hands move up to my shirt, and he tugs it off and over my head. The ache between my legs builds as he runs the backs of his hands over the top of my breasts. And while it feels good, I want those hands elsewhere.

After releasing a vocal breath, he lowers himself to the floor, on his knees, and regrips my jeans, pulling them down to my ankles and onto the tops of my boots. He then grabs me by the hips and buries his nose to my mound. His tongue slithers between my slit, and I have to grab his head to keep my balance. Probing my clit with the softest touch, Arrow is making me tremble all over. I huff as he moves his head back and forth, burrowing deeper in my folds.

And then, just as quickly as he started, he stops and pushes back up.

"On the bed," he says to me.

I part my lips, look down to the floor where my legs are held in place by a denim tourniquet, still heady from his teasing me.

"How?" I ask.

He swiftly moves behind me, makes a fist with my hair. "One step at a time."

He kicks the back of one of my boots, and I start shuffling along the floor. When I reach the edge of the bed, I lean forward and sit.

"I don't want you to call me master." He pulls the end of the rope over my shoulder and centers it around my neck like a tie.

"What then?"

He flicks his gaze to the side, then back to me. "I don't want you to say a word. I just want you to enjoy the experience. Now scoot back, all the way against the wall."

I inch backwards, crawling on my hands and pushing with the soles of my boots. Once I'm all the way back, he joins me, straddles my legs.

"Give me your hands."

I lift my arms and he begins to loop the rope around my wrists in a figure eight, then back up to my neck where he secures it once again. He then lifts my arms back up, securing them to the headboard.

He goes to his dresser and removes another long piece of rope, this one brown and prickly. He threads one end under my jeans and the other end over top, hooking the material and tying each end to the bedpost.

Smiling at me as he unbuttons his shirt, he seems pleased with himself. "Not as permanent as cementing you in place, but I don't think you'll be going anywhere."

I start to tell him I wouldn't have anyway, but then I remember the no-talking rule. I'm not sure if it's a hard rule or just a preference that I not speak. But I did make him a promise. And I plan to keep it.

He removes the rest of his clothes then climbs on the bed, walking on his knees until he's close to me.

His cock bounces in front of my face, and I lick my lips in anticipation.

I expect him to be rough but he isn't. He nudges himself closer to my mouth and I take him, wrap my lips around his girth. He moves in and out, leaning forward against the wall behind me. He pushes himself deep, sealing off the back of my throat, and my air supply. I try to kick my legs and he pulls out, repeating this process over and over until I learn to control my breathing, inhaling deeply as he comes out. We're like yin and yang as he fucks my mouth.

"Bite me," he says.

His voice is so low, I'm not sure I heard him right. But after several seconds, he repeats himself, louder this time.

"*Bite* me."

I sink my teeth into his flesh, but not very deep.

"Harder," he groans.

I clamp down, deeper and deeper until I fear I'll cut his skin.

He pumps softly, and his cock grazes along the edge of my incisors.

"Harder…"

Scared of hurting him, I don't know if I can go harder, but somehow I manage to tighten my jaw enough to bring him the release he needs.

He lets out several groans, and I swipe my tongue along the crown as he hardens inside me. His semen pumps out in soft, sudden bursts, and I resist the urge to gag—something that's unusual for me but expected given my loss of control.

Tears burn my eyes as he empties himself, fisting my strands tight and vocalizing his pleasure in deep growls that make me shiver.

"Let up," he finally says, clearing his throat several times.

I loosen my jaw and he pulls out of me before leaning down to kiss my lips. His tongue probes my mouth with a renewed hunger.

He buries himself between my legs next, and grabs the sides of my hips. His teeth grip my clit, and he flicks his tongue along the surface. I tense up, worried that he's about to deliver the same treatment he asked of me moments ago. But the rush of the unknown makes me tremble.

With the restraints, I'm helpless to his advances. I can't move, I can't say a word. All I can do is pull on the rope because my arms are starting to tingle.

Arrow continues to lick me as I struggle to hold back the moans, and the frustration of my helplessness catapults me over the edge. My body bucks through an orgasm that seizes me from head to toe. I huff, biting my lip to stay quiet.

A quiet that's quickly interrupted by the sound of Arrow's phone.

He seems to freeze in place as he curls his gaze up at me. He shuffles off the bed, wiping his mouth with his fingers and grabbing his pants off the floor. I watch him, fascinated, but also feeling panicked that something might be wrong.

He pulls his phone out of his pocket and answers with a swipe. "Yeah?"

I can't say that he's bringing me any reassurance as he turns his back to me and runs his hands through his hair. And the fact that he's mumbling curse words only adds to my anxiety.

"What's going on?" I ask him, totally breaking my promise.

He shoots me a look and shakes his head.

"No. Tell them to stay put and send Carlo out here. I'll be there as soon as I can. If Torrin leaves, they're to call me directly."

Arrow hangs up and steps into his jeans in a rush.

"What the fuck is going on?" I tug on the rope as he buttons up his jeans.

"Torrin is at his safe house. Alone."

Once his jeans are on, he crawls along the bed to untie the rope around my wrists.

"That means ..."

"Yes," he answers. "It's time."

Once my hands are free, I reach up to cup his face. "I'm coming."

His laughter tells me he thinks otherwise.

"I mean it."

He makes his way to the foot of the bed, leaning down to release the rope wrapped around my jeans and ankles.

"You offered yourself to me tonight. Said you would do whatever I asked."

"Under the condition that you and I stay here together. You're leaving, which means I'm off the hook."

He blows out a frustrated breath. "I don't have time to argue with you about this. You're staying here and that's final."

"I want to help," I tell him as I get myself dressed.

"You will be helping. By staying here."

He walks to his dresser and opens a drawer before removing a long knife covered in a leather sheath.

I walk to him and hold out my hand, and he reluctantly passes me the weapon. I remove the sheath and inspect the blade.

"If you leave me here alone, I will not be here when you get back."

Arrow grips the handle of the blade and carefully pries it from my fingers. "I'm not leaving you here alone. I'm not that stupid, Leigh. One of my guys is coming to stay with you."

"Carlo. I heard. Doesn't change shit for me. You leave, I leave. Simple as that."

Arrow's face clenches in anger. He jerks the sheath from my hand and slides it back over the blade.

"You're fucking impossible. How am I supposed to take care of you if I let you accompany me on one of my kills?"

"Your *kills*? That's what you call them?" Waves of excitement ripple through me. I know it's sick, but I can't help it.

"That's what it is." He walks across the room, steps into his boots and begins to lace them up.

I follow his lead, realizing he'll be ready to leave before me if I don't hustle.

"Your *kills*. That's really hot."

He looks my way, flicks his gaze over me with hesitation in his eyes. "You can't allow emotion to enter the equation, Leigh. This is a job that requires focus, discipline, and a clear head."

"I know that. I can do that, Arrow." I wrap my arms around his waist, bore my gaze into him. "Let me be there, show you how disciplined I am. I'll do whatever you say. I just want to be a part of it. He tried to kill me too, you know."

Rolling his head back and shifting his focus on the ceiling above, he seems to be giving it some thought.

"This is important to me. After everything I've been through, you should know that."

He pulls in a steadying breath and closes his eyes for a moment. He clicks his jaw then looks at me. "Fine. But if I tell you to not so much as blink, you'd better listen."

I press my lips to his, smiling.

"I promise."

"Then let's hurry the fuck up before we miss our chance."

Fourteen

I hold the knife as Arrow drives, pulling it out of the sheath to examine it once again. I'm a little envious that he has something like this, though I don't know why. I've never thought about carrying around a weapon of any kind.

"Be careful with that. It's so sharp, it's likely to cut without making contact."

I angle the blade up a little as we pass under the streetlights, letting the stainless steel catch the light. "Where did you get it?"

"My dad gave it to me before he died. Used it for hunting, though he didn't do as much as I did."

I glance at him. "What do you hunt with a knife?"

"Well, he used it for skinning, gutting, that sort of thing. But some people are into knife hunting wild boar. It's pretty dangerous, though."

"Wild boar?" I ask, shuddering.

"Yeah," he answers, twisting his head to look at me. "Kind of like what we're doing tonight."

I swallowed down the nervous tension. "How so?"

"Wild boar are aggressive, but they're also highly intelligent. And they come at you with their tusks—all four hundred pounds of them."

"You think Torrin will do the same?"

"Fuck yes, he'll do the same, if given the chance."

We sit silently for a few moments, and I think about the other morning, specifically the bullet that grazed his neck. "You don't think he'll point-and-shoot instead of charging?"

Arrow tenses up, rolls his neck in several circles. "I'm not going to give him the chance." He sits for a moment, grips the steering wheel tightly. "I've had fantasies for a while now of looking him in the eye as I take him out. But the circumstances have changed. I'm going to do things a little differently, so you don't get hurt."

I touch the side of his face as he slows the car down. After pulling onto a dirt road, he flips the headlights off. Darkness falls through the pine trees that surround us, and the hum of the motor is all I can hear.

I move my hand to his thigh, grip it tightly, then navigate up to the crotch of his jeans. "I want to watch."

His pants grow larger right away, and he blows a long, hard breath through his nose. "I know, Leigh. I know."

I massage his erection for several seconds before he pushes my hand away. "As much as I'm enjoying that, I have to stay focused here."

I can feel myself getting heady, so I can't disagree with him. I need to stay focused, too.

He lifts his phone and places a call as I stare beyond the tall pines, feeling a surge of adrenaline.

"He's still alone?" Arrow asks.

I struggle to hear the voice on the other end, but the volume is too low.

"Stay put. Leigh and I are here. Keep your phone on and I'll call you when it's done."

He sets the phone back in the console and flicks on the parking lights. He inches the car forward about fifty yards or so before backing in between several trees and killing the engine.

"We're going to have to hoof it the rest of the way. It's about a half mile or so," he says as he slides a pair of black leather gloves over his hands.

That means if something goes wrong, we'll have to run an entire half a mile before we get back to the car. "Okay."

He grabs both of our coats from the back seat and passes me mine. "Stay close and do everything I say, Leigh. Move as quietly as you can."

I nod, too nervous to speak at this point.

He opens the glove box and riffles around, removing a box and opening the lid. "If something happens to me, use this if you need to. Don't think. Just … point and shoot, as you say."

He drops some bullets into a small, old school handgun and flicks on the dim interior light before holding it up for me to see.

"You ever shoot a gun?"

My heart skips a few beats. "No. Never."

"Well, there's not much to it. This one doesn't have a lot of kick, so if you need it, you should be fine. Just pull the hammer back here," he says, tapping the curled piece of steel, "and shoot. You have to cock the hammer with each pull of the trigger."

He passes me the handle and I take it, feeling my hand sweat against the cold wooden grip.

"Keep it pointed to the ground at all times. And if you need to use it, aim for the chest. That'll be much easier to hit than his head."

I feel my pulse jump, and I wonder why he's trusting me with this, and why he doesn't carry it himself. But I know he has his reasons, and getting into them right now is not the best plan.

Not only that, I'm not sure I'm capable of pointing a gun at a stranger and pulling the trigger. "Arrow? I don't know if I can do it."

I twist the handgun, keeping the muzzle pointed away from us.

He wraps his fingers around the muzzle and holds it still. Then he lifts my chin with his other hand. "If he's coming at you, I promise, you'll be able to do what it takes."

The reality of this hits, and something in me clicks. I lean forward and kiss him, and he clasps the back of my head, pulling me close. He holds me like that for a moment, then bumps his forehead to mine. "We gotta roll."

I take a deep breath as I step out into the night air, tugging my coat on and zipping it up. This is one of the coldest nights we've had in a while, but what we're about to embark on makes it feel colder. I shiver and lower the gun as I follow Arrow. I barely catch him flit his fingers at me to get closer, so I walk up behind him and grip the grainy fabric of his coat.

The air feels cold against my nose and my lungs. I wish I'd worn a hat, maybe one of those ski masks, the kind that really makes you look like a crazy criminal. Then I hope that we won't be here long enough for it to matter.

We move at a slow pace for about ten minutes. The wind picks up and Arrow pauses, looks around. He turns his head and peers over his shoulder at me as I burrow close to his back. He says in a low whisper, "My men are here, but they're keeping an eye out behind the house. If you see any movement, tap my shoulder, okay?"

"Yeah," I whisper back.

My eyes immediately begin to dart around us. Waves of fear wash over me, and I grip the gun's handle, inching my thumb over the hammer in a reflex.

Then finally, up ahead, I see a house. Smoke billows from a chimney, ribbons of white being pushed aside as it wafts from the roof.

Arrow slows down, then pulls me behind a tree and holds his hand up, telling me to *stay*.

I press my hands up against the bark and watch his figure gracefully edge to the side of the house. I can't tell what he's doing, but I think he's trying to look through one of the windows. After several minutes, I see him duck low to the ground before standing back up and heading my way.

When he gets to me, he pulls me close and presses his lips to my ear. "If things go as planned, I'll finally have my revenge in a matter of minutes." He cups my face and kisses me. "I'm fucking glad you're here, sharing this with me, Leigh."

My lips spread wide in a smile as I search for his eyes in the dark. "Me too."

He flicks his head as we approach the house. I stay planted to his back, and as we get close, the front door comes into view. He lowers himself to the ground, and I follow, settling on my knees.

He reaches into his coat pocket, removing the hunting knife and sliding the sheath off the blade. He tucks it inside his coat, then roots around in his other pocket. "Your aim any good?" he asks me.

"I played basketball in middle school one year."

He holds his hand up for me, opens the palm. "Here. Aim for the doorknob."

I set the gun down in the leaves and swipe some rocks from his hand, pulling in a rush of air. They're not huge but they're not pieces of gravel, either.

I can't see the doorknob for shit, but I lift my right arm and throw as hard as I can, aiming for where the doorknob should be.

I hear a light tap as the rock hits the side of the house.

"Good," Arrow mumbles. "Again."

I throw another one, and this one I think is closer to the mark. It sounds deeper, more solid, as it strikes.

"One more," he says.

I scoop up the biggest rock I have and hold it steady as I rise up on my knees. I lean to the side and put some force behind it, launching it like it's a softball and I'm going for an out.

It makes a loud cracking sound as it strikes with force, and I do a downward jab.

Arrow and I both laugh softly, and he whips his head back at me and nods his approval.

When the front door opens, my smile quickly diminishes. It creaks loudly as the interior light cuts through the darkness. I throw my hand on Arrow's shoulder, give it a squeeze.

Fear grips me, and as he stands up, I feel around for the gun in the leaves. When my fingers touch the muzzle, I pick it up and stand up behind Arrow, pushing up on my knee with one hand. My fucking leg is asleep, and I end up wincing as I try to secure my footing.

"Stay here," he grumbles softly, taking a few steps forward.

My heart drums in my chest as Arrow gets closer to Torrin.

My thumb stays pressed against the hammer as Arrow drops the long blade to his side.

I don't know what I expect to see, but I'm sure there's about to be a confrontation.

When he's about twenty feet away from the front of the house, Arrow pauses, lifts his arm.

And that's when Torrin sees him, jerking as he recognizes his enemy.

In one fell swoop, Arrow flings the blade so hard and so fast, it goes from hand to chest in an instant. Torrin lurches backward, stumbles against the frame of the door.

He glances down, sees the knife protruding from his center. Even from this distance, I can see the dark spot forming on his shirt.

Arrow stands motionless, confident in his work.

But then Torrin reaches around to his back, and an object comes into view. An object that looks similar to the one in my grip.

He lifts the gun with a visibly weak arm and Arrow turns on his heels as I point my gun at Torrin. I take a step forward just as Arrow darts in my direction.

I pull the trigger the second I see the top of the muzzle line up with Torrin's chest, and it sends him reeling back a second time.

His left shoulder slams into the doorframe.

And he drops to the ground right as Arrow reaches me.

He spins to look at Torrin as I stand paralyzed. Waiting to see if he will get up.

"Fuck," Arrow mutters. "Oh *fuuuuck*."

I tighten my grip, cock the hammer again.

And when Arrow runs to Torrin, I stand my ground, silently still, watching my breath float out in front of me in puffs of white.

Arrow drops to the ground when he reaches Torrin's body, and that's when I come out of my trance. I start to move towards him, slowly at first. My legs feel like wobbly putty. Arrow spins his head in my direction, and I move faster, until I'm running and the wind is whipping up behind me, blowing strands of hair in my face.

I slam to a complete stop, staring down at Arrow hovering over his enemy.

"He's dead," Arrow says.

My body freezes to solid ice, then ripples of warm trickle through my veins. I finally look down at Torrin, and I see his face, frozen with eyes peeled ahead, mouth open. Blood is trickling down the side of his body from the knife. I don't see a bullet wound.

"Did you kill him? Or...?"

"Yes. I killed him. Dead ... fucking ... *on*," he says, pointing at the blade. He grips the handle, removes it from Torrin's chest, then stands up, tucking the blade under his armpit before swiping it clean. "We have to get out of here. Now."

I'm still staring at Torrin, wondering why I'm unable to pull my eyes from him.

"Leigh?" I look at Arrow and a smile begins to spread along his face. "We fucking did it."

His eyes are lit, so bright, so happy. I glance at the blade, reach forward and take it from his grasp. I sniff it, and Arrow watches me, seemingly mesmerized. It smells like copper and steel, like pennies in a jar. I tuck it inside the coat of his jacket, sharp end first, then check my hands for blood.

Nothing.

"Come on, Leigh. We have to blast." He turns from me, but I grab him by the jacket. I pull his body to mine and slam my lips to his. He pulls in a rush of air, his hands still at his side. But then he starts to melt into the kiss with me, wrapping his arms around my waist.

I drop the gun and move my hand to his crotch, feel the erection starting. "Leigh," he growls.

"Fuck me," I snap. "Do it now."

I push the bottom of his coat out of the way and start to undo his pants. "Shit," he whispers. "You're fucking crazy, you know that?"

"Crazy enough for you to fuck right here?"

He answers me by vibrating all over, or at least that's how it feels. I get lost in a mess of arms flying, clothes tearing, as he tugs my pants to my ankles and spins me around, slams me up against Torrin's house.

He enters me hard, fast. I hold on tight, feeling the adrenaline hum as it spreads through my body. I feel more alive than ever, like every cell in my body has regenerated and doubled in strength. Like I could take on the world, take on anything, and come out unscathed.

I see Torrin's body on the ground, and I think, *he did that. For me.*

Even though he didn't. And I know that on some logical level, but it doesn't change my state of mind at the moment. He would have killed Torrin with or without me and my story.

It doesn't change my state of mind or the way my body responds. I come as Arrow fucks me next to his dead enemy. We're both feeling the same thing, maybe me a little more than him. And that's when I realize I'm just as hideous as he is, but on the inside.

I don't notice when Arrow comes, but I feel him slide out of me, and suddenly he's tugging my pants back up to my waist.

"Let's go," he commands.

And now, I'm ready.

He calls his contact here on the property, tells him it's done and to get the fuck out of dodge.

We start running, but then I remember the gun, so I have to spin around and go back for it. When I do, I glance at Torrin once more, and I notice the red circles bubbling from his chest wound.

Arrow grabs me by the coat, muttering another "let's go," and we run the whole way back to his car, my lungs icy cold from the damp air, and my body shaking from the high.

He doesn't say a word as he starts the car and pulls back onto the dirt road. I can hear him breathing, though. And I can feel his adrenaline.

"We're going to have to leave now. You know that, right?"

I look his way, and he's rolling his fists over the steering wheel. "Isn't that what we're doing?"

He shakes his head. "Leave the country."

I have to let that one sink in for a minute. "You're serious? You're really fucking serious?" I ask him. The tires skid on the pavement as he turns on the main road.

"Yes," he answers. "I'm really fucking serious, Leigh. What the fuck did you think would happen once I killed Torrin? You don't think his men will seek retribution?" I can feel him looking at me, but I'm too busy staring at my hands that just pulled the trigger on a man who wanted to revenge-kill me.

I start to tremble, thinking that I made a mistake. That it wasn't supposed to be like this.

That's why he brought his luggage with him when we left his house earlier. He had said it was to take back to his buddy's house, but that was a lie.

"Why didn't you tell me?" I push my hands under my legs trying to still them, feeling my insides twist.

"Oh Jesus," he grumbles. "Would it have made a difference?"

I can't answer. I don't even know if it would have made a difference.

Arrow reaches over to me, puts a hand on my leg. "It's up to me to decide what you need to know and when you need to know it."

"No, it's not. That's not your decision to make, god damn it."

"When it involves my future and your safety, yes, it most certainly is my decision to make. I can't risk a fuck up. I took a major risk letting you come here tonight. I should have taken you to Trinity's, picked you up on the way to the airport."

"So you *did* plan to leave the country all along."

I hug my waist, feeling like I'm going to be sick. And thinking that maybe he's right. I shouldn't have talked him into letting me be a part of this. Now, I have to leave the only home I've ever known just because I was part of a crime I'm not sure if I committed or just witnessed. I'm not even completely convinced Torrin is dead.

My mind is reeling. I feel like I've been tipped over, throttled end over end in the opposite direction from what got me here in the first place. Maybe I can spin until I'm righted back to where I started.

"Take me home," I say, slumping down in the seat.

"What?" he asks, tossing his head in my direction.

"You heard me. Take me home, leave me there. I'm not doing this."

He breathes out with so much force, it makes me feel as though I'm acting like an impetuous child. "You know I can't do that. Why are we back there again?"

City lights come into view up ahead. Golden arches greet us and a plan forms.

"Just ... pull in here and let me get a coffee."

"Fuck, that's a good idea. I'll hit the drive-through and we can both get one. Gonna be a long night."

"No," I snap. He pulls into the parking lot, and the smells of grilled burgers and fries waft through the vents, making my nausea worse. "I want to go inside. Just park. Please."

I see him shake his head out of the corner of my eye. "Leigh, I can't—"

"Just park!" I scream.

He hits the brakes and turns to look at me, narrowing his brow in a blend of confusion and anger.

I seal my eyes closed, noticing my hands are balled into fists. My chest is about to explode it's pounding so hard. I swear I'm about to have a heart attack, but I take in a deep, controlling breath and try to keep my voice steady.

"Just give me this, please, Arrow. Just give me this five minutes of freedom before you take me away from the only life I fucking know."

He leans his head back, then turns the wheel and parks in front of one of the long windows. "Okay. I'll let you have this five minutes. But I'm coming in to wash my hands."

He gets out of the car and I follow him in. Before he turns to walk toward the bathroom, I stop him.

"Hey, I need a couple bucks."

"Oh, right." He pulls out a stack of folded bills, flips through them and hands me a twenty. "Get whatever you want, and a coffee for me, black."

I nod and watch him walk to the bathroom.

I wait until the door closes completely to make my move. I glance around the small restaurant. Not too many people are here, considering it's close to ten o'clock. But I see a young couple sitting near the corner.

I walk to them, forcing a self-conscious smile across my face. The girl looks up at me first, her smile fading. "Sorry to bother you. My car broke down and my cell phone's dead. I don't suppose you'd let me use yours so I can call a friend, would you?"

She looks at her boyfriend, who's taken a sudden interest in me by the way his gaze is sweeping me up and down. She then fishes through her purse. "Yeah, sure."

After typing her password, she passes me the phone, and I smile, offer her a polite nod.

I enter Andrea's number, feeling my chest pound again. She thinks I'm visiting a family member halfway across the country. Which is just insane. Even if I was visiting a family member, we'd still be messaging each other. She'd want to know what was going on. My boss and co-workers would too.

I let my finger hover over the call button, shaking and second guessing myself. What if this is dangerous? Or what if I'm putting her in danger by calling her?

Fuck, I don't even know why I'm thinking this. I only know that something is physically stopping me from making this call. I wipe my hand down the front of my jeans and go to make the call again, freezing just like before.

All I want is to return to my old life, to wake up and find out that all of this has been a dream. So many years of it, a nightmare. Wake up and discover that my dad is still alive. That my mom never left.

That Jack had never come into my life.

And I know that I'm not going to make that call that could maybe possibly save me.

I'm tied to Arrow, for better or for worse.

I'm stuck with him.

I hit the back button, erasing Andrea's number, and pass the phone back to the girl. "Sorry. I forgot her number. Thanks anyway."

Tears blur my vision, and I wipe them away as I walk to the counter and order two black coffees to go.

———————

"Are you going to talk to me at all?" Arrow asks.

I'm not purposely ignoring him. I'm really not. I'm just ... numb. Speechless. I don't know how to find the words for what I'm feeling right now.

The best I can do is give him a shrug.

He tries to take my hand, but I pull it away.

"You haven't even asked where we're going."

He's right. I haven't. but does it matter? I'm losing everything.

I know I should have thought about all of this. I just thought it would be different. That it would *feel* different.

"Leigh," he growls angrily. "Just say something. Yell at me. Cuss me out. Fucking hit me, I don't care. It's the god damn silent treatment I can't take."

I pull in a deep breath and exhale dramatically. I'm exhausted and unable to converse.

I can hear his hands twist on the steering wheel. Then he punches it with so much force, I'm sure he's dislodged something.

I jump but I don't say a word.

"Fucking suit yourself. I'm taking you to your place. You'll need to get enough belongings to last at least six months. I'll make sure your rent gets paid while we're gone so you don't have to worry about losing your apartment or your things."

Right. As long as Torrin's men don't raid my shit, I think to myself.

When we get to my place, Arrow follows me inside to "ensure my safety." I want to say haven't you done enough? But then I remember that if it weren't for him, I'd be dead right now. How can he be my savior and the reason my life is ruined, all at the same time?

My heart aches, just being in the familiar surroundings of my home. It's going to suck leaving here for six months. Especially since I just got back. I float my gaze around the room, mentally processing what I want to grab in the few minutes I have. What's so important that I have to bring it with me?

I walk to my bedroom and get the suitcase from the closet, tossing in a few of my favorite outfits. I then head to my desk and get my laptop as well as my black leather-bound book that has all my scribbles inside.

I spin in a circle, past Arrow standing in the door frame, and I see the wooden jewelry box. I open a dresser drawer and remove a sock, then I scoop up a handful of jewelry—one of the many things my mom left behind when she split. In the pile of costume jewelry is the locket my dad gave me—the one that contains two pictures of me and him as five-year-olds. I stuff the sock full and gently place it inside the suitcase, telling myself this is only temporary. That I'll be back.

"Let's go," I finally tell him.

Once we're in the car, I feel a little lighter on the inside. And I'm grateful that Arrow isn't pushing me to talk. But I can feel the weight of his grief, and his frustration. He doesn't like wondering what I'm thinking. He's used to his women talking. And that shouldn't be hard for me to do. But suddenly it's impossible.

Fifteen

I stand on the balcony of the small home, feeling the wind whip my hair and the salty breeze kiss my skin. In the distance, a dark cloud is rolling in. Rain is coming soon, according to the cab driver that dropped us off several hours ago.

Arrow approaches me from behind, placing his hands on the railing and trapping me.

"Still mad?" he asks. There's a resoluteness in his voice, as if he dares me to say yes.

"I was never mad. Just conflicted."

It's hard for me to be mad at him when he's brought me to a tropical island. Now, we're just a couple of killers hiding from a killer's tribe. It's been eighteen hours since we left Torrin's, since I found out I had to officially leave my life behind. But here, in Costa Rica, my anger is melting quickly.

He places his hands over mine. "Manzanillo has some crazy weather this time of year. That's one of the reasons I wanted to come here."

"Because you like crazy weather?" I ask him.

He laughs softly. "Because no one would expect us to come here. And as much as I hope you love it, I'm equally hopeful we won't have to stay more than a few months."

Several raindrops patter against my face. The tropical trees ahead of us dance in the wind, looking vulnerable and full of strength all at once. I think I could hang here for a few months much easier than I could stay locked up in a dark house. Even with the clouds and the storm approaching, it feels like my skin is absorbing sunlight like a wilting flower would.

I think about all that awaits us back at home, and the possibilities of not having the freedoms I was so afraid of losing. It's not a pleasant thought.

Arrow nuzzles his nose into my neck. "I've pulled you into a dark world, Leigh. I'm not sure if you'll ever be able to forgive me."

Won't I, though? He saved my life. The life that Jack's carelessness ruined. The only alternative to all of this would have been to let Torrin live and leave the country or stay in hiding.

"We would have always been on the run, Arrow."

I twist my body around to face him, knowing that my feelings have gotten twisted and turned around for whatever reason.

Arrow cups my face, squeezes his eyes shut. "You're right. We would have. But now, instead of worrying about Torrin, we have his men to fear, maybe the law, too. Time will tell."

"Do you actually fear the law? Or is there something else you're afraid of?"

He gazes into my eyes, looking unsure.

"What are you afraid of, Arrow?"

His eyes shift to my lips, and he lowers his hands, takes a step back. "Of losing the one thing that really matters to me."

I knit my brow. "What is that?"

We all have things that matter to us, but Arrow has lost both his parents and his sister, and he has millions of dollars. Is that what he's worried about? Losing his money?

"Us."

"What?"

"You heard me."

I reach for his hands, pull them to my face, needing to feel his touch again. "You should probably know that at this point, I'm pretty much stuck to you like glue."

Pressing his teeth into his lower lip, Arrow seems to be looking at me with a certain amount of hope. "That's the thing. I don't want you to feel like you're stuck. I want you to feel free."

"Well, that will be a stretch under the circumstances," I tell him.

There's a heavy weight to his stare. And I'm not sure where this seriousness is coming from, but it feels like he's about to drop a bomb.

If he is, he'd better get it over with.

He turns away from me, heads back into our room, leaving me standing outside in the wind and rain that's falling harder now.

I follow him inside, watching him sit on the edge of the bed. I join him, feeling a tension spilling from him that scares me.

"I've been watching you for more than just a few months."

I turn on the bed to face him. "You have?"

He nods, leans forward on his knees and clasps his hands.

I don't think much of his admission, assuming that he's just getting bogged down in details.

"So, how long?"

He pulls in a long breath and snaps his head to either side, popping his neck in about twenty places. "About a year."

My eyes widen, and I immediately do a mental rewind. "A year? How the fuck ...? I didn't even know Jack a year ago."

"Yeah, I know," he whispers.

"So how the fuck did you know me? And why did you start following me?"

He looks at me, softens his expression. My heart bangs inside my chest as I wait for him to explain. And I automatically reach up to touch the collar that remains around my neck.

"You helped euthanize my dog." His voice is soft and so full of pain. And his eyes? Dark and filled with grief.

I remember Victor talking about her, and I think he said her name was Molly, not the most unique of pet names. *Molly Heath*. Shit, the name is vaguely familiar. I'm pretty good with recognizing our regular client's names. But he must not have been a regular.

"You were a client where I worked?"

He stands up and walks back to the sliding glass door that leads to our porch, pushes the screen door closed and leans against the frame. "No, I wasn't. I took her to my regular vet for shots, and then for chemo when she got sick. But the night that she took a turn, I had to bring her to your practice because all the other clinics were closed, and I didn't want to take her to the emergency clinic. That place is so cold and sterile."

I start to approach Arrow but decide to keep my distance for now. "What kind of dog was she?"

"Blue heeler. But she lacked the traditional brown coloring. She was blue with black speckles."

My hand covers my mouth as the memory of their visit comes crashing back. "I remember her. But, I don't remember you. I don't even think I saw your face."

"You didn't," Arrow says, looking my way. "You were so intensely focused on comforting Molly and making sure her catheter was in place that you weren't aware of anything else. It was ... it was touching."

"She was so sweet," I mumble, recalling her last few minutes.

Arrow had carried her in, but he's right. I didn't really notice him, other than thinking he was a damn giant. It was winter, and it had been snowing that day. He wore a large hooded coat when we let him through the private entrance of our back door and into the euthanasia room.

Her legs gave out when he lowered her to the floor. I had pushed a dog bed across the room for him to put underneath her emaciated body. She had trembled when he lifted her back up for me to scoot the soft bed in place. I remember her soft whimpers and how she seemed to barely have the energy to breathe. And I recall the way her bloodshot eyes looked up at me before taking her last breath.

God, that one sucked so hard. And I know the reason I didn't notice Arrow was because I felt so sorry for Molly that's all I could see. I can only imagine how painful these memories are for him if they're making me tear up.

"Yes, she was a sweet dog. But you were sweet, too, Leigh. I don't know if you remember, but you offered her half of your uneaten cheeseburger as her last meal."

I let out a soft laugh. "Yeah. Lunch leftovers I couldn't finish. She only ate—"

"Two bites, and then she sneezed," Arrow interrupts.

I nod, then swallow down the pain. I look at him and his gaze is pointed outside.

"So why did you start following me after that?"

He pushes his hands in his pants. "Because. The way you were with her in those last few minutes of her life..." He pauses, runs his hands through his hair. "I know you might think I'm a fucking pussy, but no one is as loyal as your dog. And you showed that loyalty back by the way you comforted her." He looks at me, and my insides stir. "I fell in love with you, Leigh."

I take a step closer to him, feeling that heaviness in my heart. "Why didn't you say something? Ask me out?"

He wipes his nose, laughs softly. "I was scared. My face." He waves his hand over his left side. "I didn't think you'd want me with this crazy mess of scars."

This is the most honest he's been with me since the beginning. And I know I should be pissed about the fact that he's kept all this a secret, but I can't be pissed at him.

This is why he's surrounded himself with people, with so many women, and men. He really has lost everyone that ever mattered. And he's terrified of being alone, though he probably isn't ready to admit that.

I place my palm over his face. "I would have wanted you," I tell him.

"Really?" he asks. He seems to be searching my face for the truth, as if he doesn't believe me.

"Well, the scars may have thrown me off for a hot minute, just like they did a few days ago. But I would have gone out with you."

He covers my hand with his, smiles at me.

"You're the only girl I've ever been afraid to approach. Your beauty, it … intimidated me."

I trace my fingers over his lips, feeling a swell of emotions stirring inside of me. I would have never guessed Arrow to be intimidated about anything.

"So I watched you from afar, and when Jack started dating you, I became enraged."

His jaw ticks once, and anger flares in his eyes. I step closer to him, lock my gaze on his lips.

"I wanted him dead, Leigh," he grumbles. "I was waiting for the opportunity to set his ass up, make him fall victim to Torrin. I *wanted* my enemy to kill him."

I crash my lips into him, and he lifts me off the floor, cupping my ass as I wrap my legs around him. My arms go around his neck, and my body ignites with lust. I can't believe how much I suddenly need this man.

He grips the back of my head, kisses my neck. "I regret waiting so long to take you. If I hadn't noticed you were being followed last week…" He growls and squeezes me to him, like he's unable to finish the thought.

"But you did find me," I tell him, pressing my forehead to his.

"And I'm not letting you go. Ever."

His mouth is on mine again, and he carries me across the room. He drops me on the bed and tugs off all my clothes. I hear the rain falling outside, the wind picking up speed and rattling the screen door.

Arrow rips off his clothes with more fervor than he did mine, and when he climbs on top of me, I eagerly spread my legs to take him in. He lets his cock dance at my entrance as a tease.

"You've made me see things differently," he says.

I throw my arms over my head and angle my hips up. "I hope that I've made you feel things differently, too."

He floats his gaze over my face, giving me a slow nod. "Fuck yes, you have."

"Does that mean you won't wait for me to call you Master?"

He slips the head of his cock inside of me, and I buck my hips. "It means that other things have become more important."

I bite my lip, throw my arms around him. "Like?"

"Like..." he says, leaning down to tongue kiss me for a few seconds. "Just having you in my life."

I smile as he pushes inside of me all the way.

Our bodies move together swiftly, smoothly, for the next hour. Or maybe two. I've lost count.

Arrow and I both come but we keep at it, for no purpose other than we can't seem to stop. He flips over, pulling me on top of him so that I'm straddling his face. He holds me there, torturing me with brutal licks of my clit until my legs are trembling. And then he tosses me back down and gets behind me, snuggle-fucking me until I'm weary.

We're treating each other like a buffet, stuffing ourselves full of one another as if we're afraid we will disappear.

And I have to admit, I fear the same thing.

I've lost the most important people in my life, too. If I lost Arrow, I wouldn't know where to turn.

———————

Later than night, we're lying in bed, both of our stomachs filled with spicy burritos I'm starting to regret having eaten.

Arrow is sitting up on one elbow watching me type a message to Andrea from a burner phone, letting her know that I will be staying with relatives for a while and apologizing for the silence.

"I can't tell her where I am, can I?"

I feel him shake his head.

I send the message and set the phone down. "If I don't tell her something, I'm afraid she'll go to the police, suspicious that something's wrong."

"You can call her tomorrow, from a pay phone, and let her know you've found your mother and want to spend time with her. The less she knows, the safer she is."

I know he's right, but there's that part of me that wants to tell my best friend the truth.

"And what about Victor? Where is he going? Will he be all right?"

He kisses my head. "Victor is going back to Romania indefinitely. So yes. He'll be fine. We can call him from a pay phone tomorrow, too. If you want."

I smile, thinking of Victor. I kind of grew to like the fucker. "Does Costa Rica even have pay phones?"

He shoots his gaze to the side. "Fuck if I know. But hey, we won't be here long. Probably need to relocate to U.S. territory in the next few months."

I roll on my other side to face him. "Back to the states so soon?"

"Back to U.S. territory, like Puerto Rico."

I run my fingers through his hair, toss a leg over his side. "I hear Vieques is nice this time of year."

"Good," he mumbles, cupping his hand over my pussy. "Let's go to Vieques, start a family."

I raise a brow at him, shocked he wants to take such a huge step so soon. "Why don't we just focus on not being found by Torrin's men."

Arrow rolls me on my back, pushes my hands out of the way as he starts placing soft kisses on my tummy. "That's fine for now," he says, gazing up at me. "But someday soon, this belly of yours will be carrying my child."

He drags his tongue over my belly button, then up my chest where he leaves a wet trail along my breasts. I know what will happen if I start to argue with him. It will turn into a tug of war with me on top for a second before he puts me back in my place. And I'm just too tired tonight. So I'll let him have this fantasy, for now.

"Whatever you say, Master.

Other books by Brittany Adams:

Sold the Master Trilogy

Dark Matter

Monster

Killer

Six Days

F*ck Club

Perfect Girl

Do Not Delete

Yin

About the Author

If you're looking for dark romance mixed with psychological thriller that gets violently blended with some sexy suspense, you've come to the right place. Brittany Adams is a commitment-phobic, music-addicted, tree-hugging vegan freak who writes dark fiction across multiple genres. Most of her stories contain elements of romance, but she prefers to let her characters determine their own ending.

brittanyadamsauthor.com

www.ingramcontent.com/pod-product-compliance
Lightning Source LLC
Chambersburg PA
CBHW051140130726
47988CB00005B/1926